CAFÉ
EISENHOWER

By the Author

Junior Willis

Café Eisenhower

CAFÉ
EISENHOWER

by

Richard Natale

A Division of Bold Strokes Books

2014

CAFÉ EISENHOWER

ISBN 13: 978-1-62639-217-5

This Trade Paperback Original Is Published By
Bold Strokes Books, Inc.
P.O. Box 249
Valley Falls, NY 12185

First Edition: November 2014

CREDITS
EDITOR: JERRY WHEELER
PRODUCTION DESIGN: STACIA SEAMAN
COVER DESIGN BY GABRIELLE PENDERGRAST

To Alan for his support and love.

CHAPTER ONE
REFRIGERATION BLUES

My suicide was supposed to be memorable, one that set tongues clucking and heads rattling in bewilderment: "Did you hear about Matt? What a shock! I can't believe he would do such a thing."

The originality and daring of my self-offing, I imagined, would have a ripple effect, potentially inspiring copycat suicides by other disconsolate souls. "Just like that Matt fellow," their friends would say, recalling the sudden head rush and chest tightening when they first heard the awful news.

Yes, the perfect suicide. In retrospect, though, what was I thinking?

I have an excuse. A very good excuse. I was not in my right mind when I came up with my airtight departure plan. I was in the throes of grief, a caterwauling, miasmic grief, in the weeks following Nathaniel's untimely passing.

Officially, I'd been in love with Nathaniel for eight years but actually since the first time I set eyes on him when I was nine years old and my brother, Ben, brought him home one weekend from college.

Nathaniel brought sense to my life. And shape. And context. Before him, living was nothing more than a jumble of days as disposable as the pages of an old calendar. I simply couldn't face going back to that colorless existence. You know the gloomy, oppressive feeling you get when you have to return to your mundane job the Monday morning after a life-altering vacation that expanded your view of the world? Well, multiply that by ten and square it, and you'll only begin to grasp how I felt when confronted by a post-Nathaniel world. The anxiety alone should have been enough to kill me.

A wise man once said that losing love was like having a window in your heart. Okay, so it was Paul Simon. Still, the grieving process is a wrenching affair and one for which I was totally unprepared. It crept up on me suddenly, as the initial numbness of Nathaniel's death was wearing off. Like a giant wave, it pulled me under only to ebb and then engulf me anew without warning—hardly the best time to be making decisions about one's future as a single man, as Christopher Isherwood once so tellingly depicted.

There is no proper way to prepare for bereavement. You can't plan the day around mourning. You can't pencil in a session during your afternoon break, or cram it into one marathon session like traffic school. It's impossible to predict what will trigger those unruly spasms of sobbing, self-pity, and depression. Logically, you'd expect that one look at Nathaniel's golden smile in a matching frame on the nightstand would be enough to set me off. Instead, it made me feel queasy; the same gut-churning nausea that overtook me whenever I heard myself talking about him in the past tense.

In a bizarre way, grief is like great sex, an all-consuming passion that takes possession of the body—complete with flailing and writhing—and refuses to loosen its grasp until it has been sated. And it's just as exhausting but without the afterglow.

Is it any wonder, then, that in the midst of all this, I decided that the only solution was to end it all in the most ostentatious manner imaginable? It was my not terribly subtle way of signaling to everyone around me that I was in pain, and when I'm in pain attention must be paid. How else could I hope to compete with Nathaniel's abrupt exit during a game of touch football—when he dropped back, cupped his hands skyward toward a spiraling pigskin, and severed his spine when he slammed into the goalpost. One quick snap and it was over. If I didn't come up with a high-drama exit strategy I risked becoming merely a footnote in the story. ("Poor, wonderful Nathaniel. What a tragic loss. Oh yeah, and his lover, Matt, killed himself a few weeks later.")

Climax. Anticlimax.

When I first saw Nathaniel's corpse lying on the schoolyard field, his eyes partially open, my initial reaction was that he was merely a simulacrum. Without breath and animation, he resembled nothing more than a celebrity impersonator or a Madame Tussaud waxwork. No, the real Nathaniel had been kidnapped without a ransom note and was being held against my will. That he was truly gone sank in slowly as friends congregated to mourn him and plan a fittingly elaborate memorial while I waited in vain for the kidnappers to call.

My unwillingness to slog on without Nathaniel would come as no surprise to anyone who truly cared about him, and almost everybody did. I called him—damn you, past tense— the Pied Piper of Port Washington, but he cut a wider swath than that. He was one of those rare birds about whom nary a single unkind word was ever uttered, even behind his back. I don't suggest that Nathaniel was without fault. But most of his shortcomings came with sober self-deprecation. Nathaniel was the first to acknowledge and even poke fun at his own foibles. I used to complain that it was hard to knock someone who always beats you to the punch, which annoyed him. But then he would joke about being annoyed, making it impossible for me to stay angry with him.

It's funny what we focus on when planning our own demise. In my case, that included how the poor schnooks who stumbled upon my lifeless carcass would react—the horror, the guilt, the recrimination. What a bizarre ego trip suicide can be. But I suppose that's part of the allure. It's the haymaker, the final scene of the tragedy in which the hero's stunned friends gather over his mangled body, curse their lack of foresight, and are ultimately moved to tears as the curtain falls.

The execution of this coup de grace required ingenuity and imagination. After all, when Juliet awakens to discover Romeo's poisoned cold corpse beside her, she could hardly be expected to drink another potion. That would be redundant, unromantic, and, frankly, just plain lazy. Instead, she unsheathes his dagger and plunges it into her breast, the perfect blood sacrifice to convey the depth of her sorrow.

Like Romeo and Juliet. That's how I wanted us to be remembered, though I would have settled for Sid and Nancy. First Nathaniel dies in a freak accident and then Matt, in the throes of profound anguish, suffocates or succumbs to exposure after sealing himself in the basement refrigerator. He is discovered naked, curled up like a fetal Popsicle. Don't laugh. Grief truly warps the mind.

My vehicle to the beyond was a double-wide stainless steel and glass fridge, the kind you find in the beverage section of a convenience store. Brand name: Digby. John Clay, one of Nathaniel's commercial real-estate clients, who was going bankrupt, had given it to him a while back. "I'd rather you have it than my creditors," Clay told him.

Nathaniel had that effect on people. Even as he was facing financial eclipse, Clay couldn't resist the impulse to give Nathaniel a gift. Digby was housed in our muggy, knotty pine-paneled basement, not an inch of which had been altered since the '60s, stocked with beers and soft drinks in every color we could find, for our weekly pinochle nights. Yes, pinochle. Sometimes two-handed. And, on occasion, canasta. Anyone can do poker or bridge.

The idea to entomb myself inside an industrial-sized refrigerator came to me in a demented flash during one of my crying jags. I was stumbling around the basement sobbing and slurping down shots of Southern Comfort with beer chasers and listening to the plaintive wailings of Morrissey during his neediest period when I arrived at the somewhat prosaic conclusion that "life is no longer worth living" and its equally trite companion "I can't go on this way." Through a blur of saline and streaming mucus, there stood Digby, his cold white lights staring at me like a fatal temptation. I conjured the image of my naked body immured in glass and steel, the chilled skin a blue-veined alabaster with twin icicle trails of tears dangling from my eyelids. Creepy and, at the same time, as captivating as a work of art, the bastard child of David Blaine and George Segal—the sculptor, not the actor.

Only a tortured soul who also happens to be stinking drunk would consider this a foolproof escape plan. Methodically, I emptied Digby out, lining the beers and soft drinks in neat rows on the linoleum, sorting them by label. I suppose I went to all this trouble for the same reason that people put on clean underwear before they jump in front of a bus. With great difficulty, and a screwdriver, I removed the shelves. Stripping down, I carefully folded my clothes, laid them on the card table, and climbed in.

Here's where my nifty little scheme began to go awry. I couldn't get the doors shut. No matter how I contorted myself, a wayward limb or buttock protruded. I had miscalculated Digby's depth and height. Even in my pronounced state of inebriation, I grasped that suffocation would be impossible if I couldn't close the doors tightly. Another complication: The doors opened outward and had no inside latch.

The second alternative, death by exposure, would take far too long, especially given the level of alcohol in my blood and Digby's mediocre cooling mechanism, another factor I should have taken into consideration before emptying him out and dismantling his innards.

Knee deep in misery and self-reproach, I threw myself onto the scratchy wool plaid basement sofa and contemplated a bleak future filled with sadness and memories of Nathaniel made all the more painful by the realization that there would be no further memories of Nathaniel, someone who'd been a vital part of my life since the day he walked through the front door of our house trailing Ben, who was home for Easter recess during his freshman year at Penn.

With that petulant scowl on his face, Ben brusquely introduced Nathaniel to my mother, who giggled demurely and, rather oddly, curtsied. "So you're the great Nathaniel my Ben just can't stop talking about," she said in some inexplicable Southern drawl like she was channeling Amanda Wingfield in *The Glass Menagerie*. Ben shifted nervously from foot to foot and forced his mouth into a pained smile. Then, without so much as a glance in my direction, he flipped his hand and said, "Oh yeah, and that's the kid." Ben never referred to me by name. It was always the kid, the brat, and when he was really cross, fuckface.

When I looked up at Nathaniel, I couldn't quite make him out. His head was tilted away from me, so all I saw was this long neck and squared-off chin. Then he pivoted gracefully on his right foot and bent over at the waist until we were face-to-face. Separately, his features were somewhat exaggerated: a wide mouth with a droopy lower lip, a long, skinny Russian nose with two ski bumps and slightly flattened at the tip, flying saucer ears, and oval jade-green eyes trimmed with impossibly long silver lashes recessed under a protruding brow—all of it surrounded by a halo of strawberry curls that gradually relaxed and darkened over the years to the color of caramel toffee. When you put all the pieces together, however, he was stunning, and his face glowed with an inner spiritedness apparent even when he uttered something as casual as "Hey, kid."

I picked up on something else too, though at the time I couldn't possibly have put it into words, a strain of Slavic melancholy that grounded him and gave him emotional heft.

I'm not certain when I took my next breath, but the moment remains fixed in time like an artifact preserved in amber. Only one other memory from my childhood is as vivid and that was when Tommy Horchow pitched me high during a game of stickball and popped me right between the eyes. I don't remember it happening, only seeing stars—yes, you actually do see stars!—and waking up in the curb with my mother pressing a cold cloth against my forehead. The impact was exactly the same, except I didn't have a headache for two days after meeting Nathaniel.

He and my brother spent the Easter recess cruising around town in Nathaniel's refurbished eggplant-colored '57 Plymouth convertible or behind closed doors in Ben's bedroom blasting the stereo. From my room on the other side of the wall, I absorbed the muffled vibrations of the Stones, Cream, and Zeppelin, and—new to me—the voices of their progenitors, the holy trinity of Robert Johnson, Muddy Waters, and Howlin' Wolf.

My tin-eared brother, who thought Howlin' Wolf and Wolfman Jack were the same person, pretended to groove on it all, but I'm sure it was only to impress Nathaniel. What a wiener.

After they went back to school, I snuck in and borrowed the LPs from Ben's room, from which I was forbidden, and could soon croon passing-fair Long Island white-boy renditions of "Kindhearted Woman Blues" and "Spoonful," though the world is a better place that my "Hoochie Coochie Man" never made it beyond the confines of the shower stall.

Whenever Nathaniel visited during Ben's junior and senior years, we rarely spoke. I mostly shadowed him from the periphery, quietly feasting on his opinions about music, literature (Roth, sí; Vonnegut, no. Kerouac, self-indulgent and undisciplined; Ginsberg, heady), movies (Bergman, overrated. Godard, pedantic and bourgeois. Truffaut, Rossellini, Visconti, Ford, and Welles, all sublime), and politics (the implacability of America's ruling class and how it has undermined the possibility of true Democracy).

The little I actually grasped was thrilling. But what most impressed me was his sense of humor. Nathaniel's anecdotes had an artful rhythm. They built slowly as he drew together seemingly unrelated snippets of information, eventually dovetailing and concluding with a deliberately tossed away capper or punch line. His stories induced not just chuckles, but doubled-over holding-your-stomach howls. Nathaniel was gifted with the impeccable timing of a true raconteur which cannot and should not be attempted by amateurs. Whenever I was dumb enough to repeat one of his gems, I was usually met with blank stares and, a couple of times, alarm.

Part of my fascination with Nathaniel, I suppose, was latent sexual yearning. Or maybe not so latent since I knew I was a 'mo in the making early on, even if I wasn't quite sure exactly what that entailed except being more interested in boys than girls. But I also had a sincere desire to actually get into Nathaniel's skin, to wrap it around me like a shaman donning the pelt of a sacred animal in order to inhabit the beast's spirit. I'd never met anyone who took such exquisite pleasure in being himself as if he'd been given a choice of identities at birth and proclaimed without a moment's hesitation, "Oh Nathaniel, definitely. That's who I want to be." And he never regretted it for one moment. The Nathaniel I fell in love with as an adult proved to be plagued by many of the same doubts and insecurities as the rest of us, but even then he coped with them gracefully.

Abruptly, the winter after Ben graduated, Nathaniel disappeared from my life. My brother moved on to Yale Law and his friendship with Nathaniel was replaced by serial relationships with a long line of almost-but-not-quite fiancées, pretty much the same cute, fair-haired, slim-hipped *shiksa*, with vaguely the same name—Mandy, Sandy, Trish, Trudy.

I later learned that Nathaniel had moved to Manhattan, where he got involved in commercial real estate. After knowing her for only several months, he proposed to a woman improbably named Rosalinda. "I married a girl out of a Billy Joel song," he used to laugh. The union was short-lived and soon after his divorce, he threw himself a huge coming-out party, this being the '70s and New York and all.

At about the same time, I was battling puberty, the creator's idea of a really sick joke. Tell me, why acne? And what's with the freak-show aspects such as various parts of the body growing at different rates? For the longest time, I remained five foot two with short, slightly stubby legs as my arms shot out simian-like from my shoulders. Until I was seventeen and my legs finally grew under me, I resembled a chimpanzee with zits. I have pictures.

Shortly after my fifteenth birthday, my mother succumbed to a second bout of breast cancer. Dad was living on the other coast with wife number two or three by then, and I guess she laid down the law, because I was soon tossed from the frying pan into a boarding school in Colorado, the notorious Willow Ridge. Put seven hundred hormonally enraged teenage boys on a remote mountain top and you get more perverts—not a word I toss around casually, mind you—per square inch than anywhere outside of a federal penitentiary. Think *The Shining* with perpetual hard-ons.

For a time, I kept the priapic sociopaths at bay by blasting Tom Waits, Patti Smith, and very late Miles Davis, from his really irritating druggie phase, on my stereo. I retreated into dark corners and tried to appear very mysterious, by which I mean devoting myself to the works of Conan Doyle, Christie, Chandler, Hammett, and my favorite, Highsmith. But I soon realized that the best way to keep from being serially assaulted, especially during the cabin fever months, was to seek out an intimidating patron. Harold had football field–wide shoulders and could be fearsome, though at heart, he was one of the gentlest souls I've ever known. He said he liked "bunking" with me because I was "exotic." I never asked him to elaborate. He's married now, has three kids and lives in Bakersfield. Sends the same Christmas card every year, a snowy Nativity scene. The word Christmas is crossed out and what I'm sure is supposed to be Chanukah is scribbled in. Anyway, it's the thought that counts.

College (Vassar) was pretty uneventful after that: freedom, boyfriends, heartache, and no idea what to do with a liberal arts degree after graduation.

Cut to the night of June 24, 1983, which for me exists in the eternal present. I am working on my master's degree in education, which will eventually lead to an illustrious career teaching second grade in the Long Island Public School system. At the time, however, I envisioned a more prestigious future in academia, tooling around the quad in tweeds redolent of honey-scented pipe tobacco in the company of adoring young men hanging on my every word.

It's a Friday night and I'm on the prowl. The time is approximately ten thirty p.m. I'm playing pinball and nursing an Amstel at the Hammer in Upper Manhattan, one of those sawdust-on-the-floor bars with a strictly disco diva jukebox favoring the likes of Thelma Houston, Gloria Gaynor, and Evelyn "Champagne" King, whose "Shame" is currently holding sway. I happen to glance down the bar, where I see a dead ringer for Nathaniel hunched somberly over a margarita, and completely lose interest in pinball.

I tell myself, Matt, stop. Nathaniel is not gay. Besides, this guy's hair is shorter, darker, straighter, and he's heavier, though in all the right places. Let me be clear. I had only fixated on Nathaniel intermittently since I last saw him and then only as an idealized fantasy figure. We all have one of those lying around somewhere in our unconscious. I don't want to give the impression that I'd been harboring some twisted slasher-pic obsession.

I walk back and forth along the bar until I'm reasonably certain it's not his doppelganger. Even then, I hesitate. What if Nathaniel's not out yet and freaks because I've recognized him? What if he blows me off brusquely, or worse, tactfully with big globs of pity in his eyes? Ouch. What if everything I admired about him was merely a childhood delusion, and he's actually a raging asshole? Beware of falling idols. But if I don't make my move now, he might get up and leave, or worse, given how unbelievably yummy he is, start talking to someone else.

Fortunately, the aforementioned melancholy has cast a spell over him this evening, and he is remote and inaccessible. The stool beside him becomes vacant. In my haste to claim it,

I slip on the sawdust and nearly break my neck. Then, after I catch my breath, for the first time in my life, I say something completely idiotic that miraculously comes out right. "Nathaniel, would you mind terribly if I held your hand?"

He looks over and tilts his head back slowly. I notice the onset of a bemused grin. His eyes are saying, *I don't know who you are, but there is something familiar about you so, okay, I'll play along.* He reaches out, clasps my sweaty palm, and lifts my elbow onto the bar as if we were about to arm wrestle. The heat of his skin and the strength of his grip almost make me swoon, and I'm not an easy swoon. He pulls closer, chuckles, and shakes his head. He still can't make the connection: a former trick, an old business acquaintance?

"I'm sorry. If I'd met you before, I don't think I'd forget," he says. How is it possible for one person to always know the perfect thing to say in any given situation? It's like he has a team of the best writers on call in his brain 24/7.

When I tell him who I am, he shakes his head and exclaims, "Wow! Really?" He gives me the full-body scan, head to toe, looking for some remnants of "the kid." At the same time, he is seriously checking me out. Without letting go of my hand, he says, "Let's go somewhere, Matthew."

I assume this means unbridled, passionate sex until dawn. I follow him in my car all the way back to Long Island guessing that we're spending the night at my place. He pulls into one of those harshly lit always open diners, where we play catch-up. Ben is only mentioned in passing to confirm that, indeed, he and Nathaniel drifted apart as college buddies sometimes do, especially when one of them is closet jumping. When he asks after my brother, I say that between the grueling hours he puts in at that stick-up-the-ass Manhattan law firm he works for and his serial girlfriends, I rarely see him. And anyway, we were never really close.

Nathaniel sketches out the details of his failed marriage: It was Rosalinda who broke the news that he was gay and should stop wasting her time and his own. They separated amicably, and he engaged in a noble struggle between coming out and becoming a full-fledged alcoholic. "I know some guys can do both, but I lose focus when I try to do more than one thing at a time," he says. He has recently moved to Port Washington, where he's supervising renovations on a fixer-upper his grandfather left him, a large, rambling three-story clapboard with a wraparound porch, which he is painting forest green with the palest lilac trim. He's thinking of maybe living there when it's finished.

When it's my turn, I do my best to amuse him—okay, impress him—by cherry-picking the most lurid episodes from my years under lock and key at Willow Ridge, tales of messy teenage lust in close quarters. He seems keenly interested, even tickled. Either that or he's just feigning interest because he's projecting forward to when we're both naked and rolling around playing pretend wrestling. As we both start to wilt under the combined weight of beer, the diner's interrogation room fluorescent lighting, and the fact that it's four o'clock in the morning, he lets go an enormous yawn and says, "Matthew, my man, I'm beat. Time to call it a night."

What I hear is rejection, and the butterflies of anticipation in my stomach collide and collapse into a heap. His intentions are strictly honorable, dammit. Or maybe I'm getting the brush-off because he still sees me as Ben's kid brother. Worse, he considers me a flighty party boy and is trying to get away as quickly as possible without appearing rude. That's the trouble with born charmers. They can totally snow you and you still blame yourself.

Nathaniel reads my disappointment. I'm a terrible actor. Pauly Shore terrible. He leans over and daubs a kiss across my cheek. "Let's continue this tomorrow night over dinner." That's what he said. I remember it distinctly.

My first impulse is to yell, "Oh boy, you bet!" Instead, I take a deep breath and say, "Sure. I don't have any plans," with just the right touch of blasé. Then I remember that tomorrow night is Saturday. Dimwit. Well, too late to take it back now.

We shake hands in the parking lot and glance back at each other as we get into our cars. On the drive home, I give myself a thorough reality check. Look here, mister, you're getting way ahead of yourself. Dinner may just mean dinner. So stop behaving like a crazed teenage girl at a Rick Springfield concert. Or he may want to feed you, bed you, and send you on your way. What of it? For all you know, he's a total dud in the sack, has intimacy issues, or is consumed with self-loathing. You name it, you've dated it.

By the time I get home, I'm completely sober and calm. I do not sleep a wink.

❖

As I dressed for our date, I promised myself I was not going to fall apart if he expressed no interest in an after-dinner brandy and some fellatio. Since it was unofficially a first date, I couldn't very well pounce, or he'd think me immature or worse, wanton. If all went well and he asked me out again, I'd casually accept. And then, if he still didn't put out, swallow hard and shift gears into let's-just-be-friends.

Four dates later—wonderful evenings with lots of laughs and never a single uncomfortable lapse in conversation—we were nestled in the back row of a movie theater. I have no idea what we went to see because we were so busy making out and groping one another like love-starved teenagers. All that was missing was a popcorn tub with a false bottom. Then he excused himself to go to the men's room and didn't come back. After waiting impatiently for a full half hour, I found him in the parking lot walking around in circles. What followed was a display of Matt's homegrown fireworks. Not pretty. But very noisy.

Nathaniel reacted like I'd shot his dog. When I finally ran out of cherry bombs, he said quietly, "I think I'm falling in love with you. And that's kinda new and scary for me." Now it was my turn to be stunned into silence, which he interpreted as indifference.

Perhaps I should explain. All the pre-adolescent fantasies I'd harbored for Nathaniel were largely hero worship. He hero. Me worshipper. I was still woefully immature and groin-centric, so it was hard for me to think much past a satisfying roll in the hay or a torrid affair that would end disastrously, as they always do. When he said "falling in love," I suddenly came down with a bad case of "Oh my God, he thinks of me as an adult and now I have to behave like one." We all say we want to be treated like grown-ups. We rarely mean it.

No words were exchanged on the ride home, and I ran out of the car without even saying good night.

The next three weeks were torture, yank-out-the-fingernails torture. Like a little brat who claims he wants his parents to stop infantilizing him, I became indignant and childish. Who the hell does Nathaniel think he is saying he's in love with me? Malarkey. I know when I'm being set up for the big fall. Unlike in the movies, love doesn't always lift you up into the ether. So I resolved to move past Nathaniel. Nathaniel? Nathaniel who?

Shifting deftly into self-preservation mode, I chose to distract myself with any number of willing candidates. One night, after an extended and what I would categorize as a more-than-satisfactory encounter, I abruptly kicked the unsuspecting schmuck out, sucked down two whiskeys, neat, and at around three in the morning, dialed Nathaniel's number and confessed to his Mr. Rogers–like voice recording, "I just called to say that this is unchartered territory for me too."

Nothing is more terrifying than hearing the sound of your own vulnerability surrounded by silence. As I was hanging up, I heard a slight click on the other end and some fumbling with the receiver. After what seemed like two and a half years, I heard a groggy rasp. "I understand."

"Next step?" I ventured, knees knocking together.

"We run the risk of being totally devastated."

"Right now that would be an improvement for me."

"Ditto."

I love that he said "ditto."

"How about we get together for breakfast?" I asked.

"What time?"

"Now."

"Where?"

"You know."

And I love that he knew exactly where "you know" was. When I arrived at the diner, he was sitting at a table in the window under a glaring neon sign waiting for me.

CHAPTER TWO
ONIONSKIN

After that abysmal attempt at asphyxiation in my knotty pine-finished basement, my decision to take a sabbatical and traipse off to Eastern Europe in the dead of winter to claim an unexpected inheritance might appear almost rational. All I had to do was show up in person to claim it. What could be easier? Even Caroline didn't think it was a bad idea, which was weird. Like me, she regards any point beyond the tri-state area as uncharted wilderness.

Caroline's been my bosom buddy since college. We both teach at Gibbons Elementary. I'm second grade, she's fifth. Caroline is the only person who knows about the fridge fiasco. When I phoned her afterward, hysterical, she simply said, "that is so you," and came by to help me put the shelves and my nerves back together.

Because she is such a good friend, Caroline indulges my lunacy, always giving me enough rope while at the same time quietly but firmly holding on to the opposite end. Everyone should have a Caroline in their lives. When I introduced her to Nathaniel, after only fifteen minutes in his company, she took me aside and asked why I would hesitate for a second to commit to him. "That's like getting a complimentary gold bar for visiting Fort Knox and saying 'Thanks, but everything else in my house is silver.' Well, I say throw everything out."

After Nathaniel died, Caroline was the only one of my friends who didn't expect me to get on with my life after some arbitrary suitable period of mourning. She didn't chew me out for my failed suicide attempt or treat me like I was mentally unbalanced. No, she was her usual pragmatic self. "Look, we all deal with this stuff in our own way, though grief counseling might have been a preferable option. That being said, I realize that I'm only standing next to your shoes, not in them."

Gotta love her for that.

Caroline even indulged my sudden mac and cheese addiction, when for a solid month I ate nothing but—morning, noon, and night. As a mark of solidarity, she joined in my comfort food crusade, which I found very comforting. When I first told her about my plan to travel to a city I'd never heard of, in a country about which all I knew I'd learned from *Jeopardy*, she didn't even blink. "Sounds like a great way to broaden your horizons," she said, coiling a strand of hair tightly around her right index finger. It's just one of her many an endearing little-girl tics that, if I was straight, would be a total turn-on. Reminds me of Carroll Baker in *Baby Doll*. But then I'm all for sucking your thumb well into adulthood, though perhaps not in public. As a pacifier, it's preferable to alcohol and drugs and much easier on your pores and internal organs. The only downside is the potential for an overbite.

But back to the former S.S.R. "I'm just curious," Caroline asked. "You think that retreating behind the Iron Curtain in the middle of winter is the best way to get out of your funk?" she asked.

"It's worth a try." I shrugged. "Anyway, I don't think I have much choice. The finger of fate is pointing me east, and I'd be a fool to ignore my destiny."

Two weeks earlier, a letter addressed to my late mother arrived at the house in which I was raised and lived in until

I was sent off to boarding school. The two-story clapboard in Manhasset had since changed owners three times. The current resident, a Mrs. Pepper, was about to toss the letter when her daughter-in-law, Hannah, picked up the crinkly, onionskin envelope and became intrigued by the underlined word "Vital" typed in the bottom right hand corner, where people sometimes write Personal or Confidential. She took it across the street to Kathy Hannigan, who has lived in the neighborhood forever, knows everybody's business, and freely shares the gory details with anyone who bothers to ask. At first she was stumped by the identity of the addressee, Anya Vrozinski, Mom's original maiden name. Her father Americanized it to Volt, which sounds a lot like a spark plug company.

"No such animal ever lived at that address," Kathy said confidently. Hannah was halfway out the door when Kathy had a change of heart. "Wait a minute. I wonder if that could be Ann Robins? I remember her saying that her family was from Poland or Russia or someplace in that general area and that her father changed their name the way people used to in those days. Anya? Ann? Possible. Poor thing died of breast cancer maybe ten years ago. She was a divorcée and had two nice boys. The older one was already on his own, but I think the ex-husband put the younger one in a private school. He'd remarried and, naturally, the new missus didn't want the first wife's kid around. What was the younger boy's name? I wish my Charlie was here. They used to play together. Wait a minute, it's coming to me. Matt. Matt Robins."

From behind her in the living room, her grandson, Jonas, looked up from his coloring book and whined, "Matthew Robins. We're not allowed to call him Matt."

The next day, Jonas walked into class with the letter pinned to the front of his shirt. He tried to get my attention, but I was busy tending to Laila, who was insisting, "I gotta do throw up."

"Are you sure, Laila? Maybe if you take deep breaths, it'll pass." Then I demonstrated. Long inhale. Even longer exhale.

She tried it. Inhale. Exhale. The urge seemed about to subside when Jonas approached and yanked at my corduroys. "Matthew. I got something for you." He poked his finger against the manhandled envelope affixed to his chest.

"I have something for you," I corrected him, "not I got."

"I haaaave something for you. From my grannndddmother."

At that precise moment, Laila barfed up her partially digested breakfast, what appeared to be Eggos and orange juice spattering the linoleum floor and my Top-Siders.

Over the next hour, I escorted Laila to the school nurse and advised that she contact the girl's mother to pick her up, told the janitor to clean the floor and deodorize the classroom, and changed into a pair of Pumas which I keep stored in my trunk alongside an extra shirt and slacks for just such serendipitous encounters with seven-year-olds.

Once puked on, twice shy.

On my way back to class, the principal, Mr. Carstairs, passed me in the hallway and looked down disapprovingly at my footwear. I was in no mood. So I snapped at him, and he scurried back to his office like a mutt who's been whacked on the behind with a rolled-up newspaper.

It took another half hour and loads of air freshener to get the kids back on track. During the entire time, Jonas did not budge. Not an inch. When I finally turned my attention to him, he was understandably annoyed. "My grandma says this letter's for your mom, who's dead."

Well, that caught my attention.

The contents of the letter were in an unfamiliar language that was, moreover, indecipherable, a continuous scrawl interrupted by peculiar punctuation marks. Nonetheless, I regarded its circuitous delivery to be of great significance, a communication from above and beyond.

"There's no other explanation for this letter," I told Caroline. "It says Vital right here on the envelope, a word derived from the Latin for 'life.'"

"You could very well be right," she replied. "But just to be on the safe side, shouldn't you find out what it says first?"

I needed a translator. Who did I know from the old country who was still alive? The only person who came to mind was Auntie Edna. But last I'd heard, she'd been shipped off to a convalescent home in Pennsylvania by her sons, who were mortified that she'd taken to wearing nightgowns all the time. She wore them at home, to the market, and worst of all, to her granddaughter Myrna's bat mitzvah. When they hinted that her recent fashion choices could be a sign of incipient dementia, she countered with a perfectly reasoned argument. "It's not as if I'm going around naked. If young ladies today can prance about in short slips, I can certainly leave the house in a floor-length nightgown."

The garments were made of heavy cotton and buttoned up at the neck, and she always wore underwear so no stiff wind could expose her to scandal. The ensembles were always smartly accessorized with matching shoes and purse as well as the diamond pendant her beloved Herbie, "may he rest in peace," had given her for their forty-fifth anniversary.

Auntie Edna reminded her sons she had worked hard her entire life in order to raise her children, a doctor, a lawyer, and a college professor—"ungrateful *pishers* whose dirty bottoms I wiped"—and thus earned the right to dress as she saw fit in her dotage.

The logic was lost on the three *pishers*, who had their mother legally sequestered in a senior development called

Serene Valley, far enough away so she couldn't wander back home. In Serene Valley, she could wear tasteful sleepwear to her heart's content without fear of disapproval or censure.

When I ran into Auntie Edna's son Phil, the doctor, at the hardware store, he assured me she didn't put up a fight. Phil is about fifty and, ever since he first heard that I was gay, has felt the need to flirt with me whenever we run into each other, sad closet case that he is.

The last time I'd actually seen Auntie Edna was at my mother's funeral. We're not actually related. I call her Auntie out of respect. She was best friends with my maternal grandmother, Esther. They were born within fifty miles of each other in the old country and were likely related. Jewish families in the region had been intermarrying for centuries.

As I was coursing along the Pennsylvania Turnpike in the driving rain, I wondered if Auntie Edna's predilection for flannel nightgowns was her only eccentricity these days, given that she was pushing ninety. The sky cleared the moment I arrived at Serene Valley, which I viewed as another portent. True to its name, the convalescent home was placid and nestled in spectacular Pennsylvania mountain greenery. The location was more like a large crevasse than a valley, but Serene Crevasse would hardly inspire confidence.

Aunt Edna no longer wore nightgowns. She was now consigned to standard issue open-in-the-back short hospital gowns, the kind designed by the medical Gestapo so that even the most exalted among us feels vulnerable and exposed. She was predictably frail, with hardly any hair left on her head except for scattered clumps of gray frizz. She rarely walked or ate much anymore, the nurses told me. "But she's still alert."

The nurses had underestimated Edna. I discovered her dozing in a metal armchair in her semi-private room and gently tapped her shoulder. "Auntie Edna, it's me, Matthew. Esther's grandson." She opened her eyes and tightened them into a squint as she traversed the rickety bridge between dreams and full consciousness. Then a beam of recognition. "Oh yeah. I remember you. The *feygele*."

"Right you are. I came to ask you a favor."

She clapped her hands together and grinned. "No one's asked me for a favor in years. What can I do for you, my dear?" I fished the letter out of my pocket and explained how I got it. "My goodness," she exclaimed. "You were obviously meant to receive this letter." She jiggled her fingers, motioning for me to hand it over. Then she pointed to the dresser atop which lay a pair of silver wire-rims. She rubbed the onionskin paper nostalgically, and her eyes welled up. "The last time I got one of these was during the Great War. After that, no more."

Then she shook off the past and put on her spectacles. "Terrible penmanship," she scoffed. "But otherwise this was written by a very well-educated person. I can tell by the vocabulary and the use of tenses. Yes, yes. It's signed Lawyer Bombyk." She read it to herself with a series of hmms, huhs, and oh mys. When she finished, she flattened the letter across her lap and exclaimed, "Young man, it seems you've come into an inheritance."

"But I don't know anyone over there," I said, incredulous.

"Apparently you do." She chortled.

Lawyer Bombyk was writing in regard to the estate of the recently deceased Leonard Baknin. In the absence of direct heirs, he had bequeathed his entire estate to my mother or her survivors. Said estate consisted of Leonard's two-unit residence, an adjacent business space and all its contents, as well as the proceeds from his savings account. Lawyer Bombyk awaited notice of receipt and correspondence from an attorney to begin settlement of the assets.

"Who the hell is Leonard Baknin?" I asked.

"What do you mean? You don't remember your uncle Leonard?" Then she smacked her forehead. "No, of course you don't. It was before your time. Leonard was Esther's younger brother. Appeared on her doorstep one day out of nowhere and went right back home right after the war to find out if anyone survived." She shook her head and sighed. "But he had to make sure."

As she talked about Leonard, I had a small epiphany. When I was a boy, my mother once told me I had my uncle Leonard's eyes. She probably told me more about him, but I guess none of it stuck. I was flattered when Auntie Edna noted that Leonard was "quite a handsome young man. The girls were thick after him. If I wasn't already married to Herbie... And industrious besides. Worked day and night. Set aside every penny for his family when the war ended." Another long sigh.

Shortly before World War II was declared, Leonard made his way into the country via Canada, traveling with a false passport using a name that was decidedly Aryan, Auntie Edna told me. The tightly knit Jewish community in Queens, many of whom had relatives who couldn't emigrate, took him in and guarded his identity. "They were afraid if the authorities found out, he'd be deported or drafted into our Army. He had to not exist," she explained.

Uncle Leonard made the most of his time in seclusion, quickly mastering both English and the joys of unfettered capitalism. "He picked up the language in no time and soon spoke with only a hint of an accent," Auntie Edna assured me. Then Rachel Miller, a family friend, lost her husband and was left with a dry goods business in lower Manhattan that she had no idea how to run. Leonard became her silent partner, operating the shop from an upstairs room.

"He was so smart, that Leonard," Edna said, lifting her eyebrows for emphasis. "In just a few months, he turned the business around and began to raise the money for two more stores. There was talk that he was handling more than the widow Miller's business," she said with a slight eyebrow raise. "But when did he have the time to fool around? He was running three successful shops during a war when there were all kinds of rationing. He was clearly a man to be reckoned with and we all predicted great things for him.

"But the minute peace was declared, he sold everything—at a very good profit, mind you. We couldn't talk him into staying, not for love or money. He invested his and Rachel's profits in bonds, leaving them both very comfortable, gave a share of his cut to Esther to thank her for taking him in, and booked passage on the *Constitution*. Your grandmother begged him not to go back. She knew what he'd find and how devastated he'd be. But the pull of family can be very strong."

Yet another prolonged sigh. Opening the trunk of mothballed reminiscences seemed to sadden and deplete her. "Forgive me, darling, I'm feeling a little weak."

I thanked her, gave her a big hug, and quietly slipped out.

"Matthew," she called after me. "If you go over there, be my eyes. And please say hello for me."

On the way back, seeing Auntie Edna in that frail and diminished state for what was likely the last time, triggered a trip down the memory highway. I was suddenly overwhelmed by loss. And this time it wasn't only Nathaniel. The last time I'd seen him alive was in every way routine. I was doing bills when he popped down the stairs, grabbed an apple from the dining room table, brushed a kiss against my forehead, and sailed out the door mumbling something about taking pork chops out of the freezer.

My melancholy was for the many other loved ones and friends I'd lost over the past few years. My mind drifted back to that last chat with Mom, just before she fell into a morphine haze. The skin on her hands and face was cool and loose fitting, as if her bones were shrinking under her. We didn't discuss anything heavy like real life, just mother stuff, the usual laundry list. Don't forget to stop the newspaper. Iron a white shirt for school. Use some spray starch, and for pity's sake how did you wear down the heels on those new shoes so quickly? After that morning, she never spoke again except with her eyes, which would follow me around the room like a child learning to see.

I was also confronted with a backlog of emotion for the scores of friends who, over the past decade, had succumbed to tortures that would have defrosted the heart of even the most malevolent sadist. Hospitals, sickbeds, memorials, Act Up protest rallies with barely a moment to properly mourn. No sooner did one friend shrivel away than he was joined by another, and another, and another. At a certain point Nathaniel and I shut down. Unable to process all that sorrow, we pushed some invisible hold button in our brains.

Now, aggravated by Nathaniel's untimely passing, the bill was finally coming due. Before getting on my case about having the luxury to grieve for my absent friends, any one of whom would have gladly traded places with me, all I can say is that I'm way ahead of you. Being merely a witness to annihilation is cold comfort. Try reconciling survivor guilt and survival instinct without seriously messing up your head, and then we'll talk.

It was during this crying jag on a remote shoulder of the New Jersey turnpike that I came up with what I regarded as another foolproof plan. I would put an ocean between myself and all those ghosts—an extended holiday in Eastern Europe to retrieve my inheritance.

But first, one final masochistic act. Since misery loves company, I decided to pay a visit to my brother Ben.

My brother and I have always been distant, in part due to the difference in our ages, but also because my birth, designed to heal my parents' growing rift, had the opposite effect. They split legally when I was four, but from the time I could walk, my existence was a nagging reminder of their failed marriage, especially in Ben's eyes.

Not that I made it easy for him. Since I only saw my father two weeks a year, and my mother was consumed by bouts of depression and successive battles with breast cancer, Ben was my only family. But the more I tried to reach out to him, the more distant he became. He did such a good job of pretending I didn't exist, he almost believed it.

Ben had just started law school when Mom made her final descent. He rushed home and maintained a solitary vigil in her airless bedroom. He was with her on the blustery fall afternoon when she passed. When I got home from school, I found him holding her hand and crying so hard he was wheezing. Sensing my presence, he turned sharply, shoved me out the door, and locked it. He stayed inside alone for the next few hours and emerged only to phone my father. At the wake, Dad and I stood on one side of the casket and Ben on the other. He didn't speak a word. The following day, he returned to school, and I was left to fend for myself in the empty house until I was spirited off to boarding school a few months later. In the interim, Dad sent me regular checks and even hired a woman to clean the house once a week.

I'm not trying to sound like an orphan of the storm here. Ours was hardly the only dysfunctional family on Long Island.

I never felt sorry for myself growing up, enduring the way kids do, only occasionally displaying the scars and then not so much to elicit pity as to celebrate my fortitude.

I didn't see Ben again until my sophomore year of college. Dad was in New York on business and invited us, separately, to dinner. I chose this already awkward reunion to announce that I was gay in vividly graphic terms. I believe it's called "acting out," which in this instance is wonderfully appropriate. Dad did the concerned parent routine, asking leading questions like "Are you sure?" "Have you at least tried girls?" and my favorite, "Is it because you're mad at me?"

As I argued with him, I heard Ben mutter "faggot" under his breath, and I jumped up from the table, screaming "Oh yeah, well how'd you like to see this faggot kick your fat ass?" A hollow threat, to be sure. Ben is six foot two and has about forty pounds on me.

"I want you two boys to get along, do you hear me?" my father reprimanded.

To which we replied, almost in unison, "Fuck you," and stormed out of the restaurant in different directions. Antipathy toward Dad was one of the few sentiments we shared.

Two weeks later, I received a note from Ben. "Sorry if I offended you. Truce?" I kept it pinned to the wall over my desk until I graduated, but never replied. My father tried to reconcile us once again by ordering Ben to attend my graduation since he was going off on a Caribbean cruise with wifey number three and would have had to forfeit every penny if he canceled.

As he walked beside me on the quad, Ben said, "I wish Mom was here to see this. It would have made her so happy." I'm not sure if he was referring to my graduation or the two of us not being at each other's throats. On the sidewalk, he shook my hand.

I said, "I'm going to kiss you on the cheek now. So please don't freak out."

The rapprochement was temporary. Not long after he found out about me and Nathaniel, he went ballistic, as in completely loco, arriving at our house under the cover of night, pounding at our front door, screaming at the top of his liquor-soaked lungs and waking up the entire neighborhood.

And here I thought I was the drama queen.

Allow me to backtrack for a moment. Early on in our "let's take things slow" phase, before we had even done the dirty deed, Nathaniel and I had a serious discussion about a problem we'd both been grappling with, which had kept us from jumping into bed, namely "the Ben thing." Nathaniel confessed to a secret crush on Ben during his homosexual panic phase. It passed, he assured me, as did the panic. Then there was the fact that I was Ben's kid brother. "And it just feels weird, because I can still picture you as a child."

Ick.

I had my own issues, like the fear I might be transferring my lack of fraternal affection onto Nathaniel. Believe me, I had no conscious desire to bed my brother or my father. But, hey, I took Psych 101 like everyone else. What if I was sublimating?

After batting the topic around, we concluded that we only had one way to find out whether these issues were genuine impediments or we were using them as an excuse to postpone intimacy. So we decided to go for it, which is a roundabout way of saying that, in the end, it was Ben who brought us together. Not that it would have mattered even if he had given us the opportunity to explain, which he most definitely did not. That night, the first words out of his mouth as we groggily opened the door were "I just want you to know I think you're both disgusting."

I could have dealt with the disgusting part. That's always been a matter of opinion. Some people think fried calves' brains are a delicacy. I'm not one of them. But my feeling is, as long as you don't force me to eat it, chow down.

"You're talking like a jealous lover," I sneered, with my infallible knack for making a bad situation worse.

Turns out Ben had come to defend my honor, which is kind of sweet in a twisted sort of way. "I want you to keep your hands off my little brother," he bellowed at Nathaniel. "He's just a kid."

Ever the pacifier, Nathaniel tried to inject some reason. "I know you find all this strange, but—" Before he could finish, Ben tackled him, flattening him against the floor. When he raised his fist in the air, I yanked back his arm before he could do any real damage. With Nathaniel's help, we pushed Ben out the door and locked it. He continued banging for a few minutes, spritzing the air with obscenities. Then he drove off and that was the last either of us saw or heard from him.

Barging into Ben's Manhattan aerie on my way home from Serene Valley was yet another grief-induced folly comparable to my wayward encounter with that uncooperative refrigerator, but I was stuck. I needed for him to sign off on the "inheritance." Ben lived in one of the top-floor apartments of a sleek glass and metal condo that was more suitable to a beachfront in Miami than a constricted corner of midtown Manhattan. Being particularly fond of the element of surprise, after locating his name in the lobby directory, I eluded the doorman and disappeared into the elevator. The young lady who answered the door was yet another replica of all the girls he'd previously dated, thin to the point of anorexia, blond and compact. This one was a bit snarky, too.

"Ben doesn't have a brother," she said. "I would know."

"It's okay, Suzie," I heard him call from inside.

Ben was at the dining room table poring over legal briefs, combing his fingers through his dark, shiny black hair, another enviable trait he inherited from Dad, along with his height, whereas I have maybe another decade before my forehead and the back of my head unite in one arid expanse.

"Hey, Matt. How's it going?" he said, as if he'd seen me earlier in the week. Okay, I thought, so that's how you want to play it.

"I've got wonderful news. We are heirs to a legendary fortune."

Ben had the good sense to laugh when I told him the story of our secret Eastern European uncle. Suzie listened to every word while pretending to be engrossed in a fashion magazine.

When he motioned me to follow him out to the terrace, her mouth got all pinched, and I knew he was in for a lashing after I left.

"So Suzie is…" I asked when she was safely out of earshot.

"Never mind Suzie," he said brusquely. "I just want you to know I was shocked when I heard about Nathaniel. I'm so sorry."

Good old Ben, still the same old button pusher. "So shocked you couldn't show your face at the memorial?" I countered.

He sighed. "I thought I'd only make things worse."

Touché.

"Nathaniel was a really important person in my life," he said.

"And that's why you tried to rip his face off."

"I was being a moron."

Long, very uncomfortable silence.

"So what about this inheritance thing?" I asked.

"It's all yours, bro. I mean, what are we talking about here? The currency in Eastern Europe is *bupkis*."

"Will you sign a letter to that effect? I'll need to present it to the lawyer when I see him."

"Sure thing. You're not actually going there, are you? 'Cause that's just crazy."

CHAPTER THREE
THE "PRESUMPTUOUS" HEIR

While fatiguing and sometimes dangerous, my multi-legged voyage was relatively trauma free, which was a surprise given that the closest I'd come to a foreign country before this was the American side of Niagara Falls. But from the moment the jet engine fumes crept up my nasal cavity, I gave myself over to a state of altered consciousness. For the next thirty-six hours, time inexplicably expanded and contracted. Spaces were extreme, either cavernous or constricting. Sounds were muffled one moment, unbearably loud the next. The sun and moon appeared and retreated at whim. Whenever I asked even the simplest direction, the transportation personnel winced and wrinkled their foreheads as if my query not only taxed their mental capacities but induced actual physical discomfort.

Airports and train stations were suffused with the aroma of strange spices and peculiar-smelling disinfectants. People emitted strange odors, sometimes fetid, sometimes overly perfumed, often both. A sandwich still looked like a sandwich, but didn't taste the same. Coca-Cola bottles bore similar packaging, but the soda was either much sweeter or merely colored seltzer. Magazines and newspapers were oddly laid out with sometimes chaotic graphics. Autos and trucks were smaller and weirdly shaped. Money came in an infinite variety of colors, denominations, and sizes, and almost no one ever had change.

During my journey, I encountered several Americans on their own wild goose chases. On the flight to Frankfurt I befriended my seat partner, Elaine, a divorcée with overly coifed dyed black hair and an unsteady smile. She claimed to be thirty-two but even in the dim cabin light, I could tell she'd shaved off at least five to ten years. Elaine was headed to Cracow to solidify her relationship with Pavel, a younger man she'd met the previous year in Paris, where he was completing his doctorate in French literature at the Sorbonne. Pavel assured her that age was irrelevant when it came to true love, and she bought it. The somber mug shot–style photo she showed me—the guy had perp written all over him—contradicted the sensitive "soul of a poet" to whom she'd given her heart. But hey, the camera and I aren't exactly the best of friends either.

They met rom-com style at a café on the Left Bank in April where Eros was testing out a new quiver of arrows. The heated affair was followed by breathless correspondence and teary transatlantic phone calls. This trip was merely a test run, she said. If they found that the magic was still there even in the depths of the Polish winter, they planned to marry in the spring, after which Pavel said he was not averse to leaving his motherland for the U.S. I stowed my cynicism in the overhead compartment for the duration of the flight and wished her all the best.

Dirk, with whom I shared a second-class compartment on the train out of Frankfurt, was blessed with the kind of blue-sky idealism everyone is guilty of at least once in their lives, usually in their early twenties, when the world appears wild with promise. He was headed to Budapest to trace his Magyar roots and improve his Berlitz-acquired Hungarian. Otherwise he had no plans, not even a place to stay. Nor did he have enough money to get back home to Rhode Island if the trip was a bust. No matter, he said. He was doing it "for the experience," a phrase no one with any serious mileage under his belt can pull off. As I watched him nap, his wide, fleshy mouth inspired my first twinge of desire in months. It wasn't so much lust as a yearning to kiss someone, which immediately brought Nathaniel to mind—and that was the end of that.

Two or three stops after Dirk detrained, he was replaced by Sam, a jovial, corn-fed Ohioan who immediately engaged me in conversation, more like a one-sided spiel. Sam's last name was Taylor, but it should have been Glick. He had been living in post–Velvet Revolution Czechoslovakia and buying up every piece of available real estate in anticipation of it becoming a separate country, the Czech Republic. After breaking off from the less prosperous Slovakia, he assured me, property values would skyrocket. Then he'd cash out and retire to a life of leisure, presumably someplace more temperate than either Prague or Xenia, Ohio. As he spoke, he tapped out a Morse code with his restless leg, and he nervously patted the money belt around his waist like he was keeping tabs on a pretty girl who was too young for him and eager to abscond with the first decent man who looked her way. After I mentioned that my recently deceased lover had also been in real estate, he turned suddenly quiet, and after that we exchanged few words.

❖

Once I'd passed out of Germany, the vivid and sometimes lush countryside grew increasingly desolate and colorless and sparse until the landscape was a fuzzy black and white, bleary and out of sync like a worn 16 mm print. On the side of the tracks, broken, abandoned machinery lay defeated beside hollowed-out stone or concrete structures. The starkness reminded me of Bergman's grimmer films or early Polanski, but without the lyricism and lucid cinematography.

The farther east I traveled, the more outmoded and unreliable the transportation and amenities. It was as if I'd ventured into a parallel present in which the world had remained in stasis for the past half century, slowly ground to a halt, and begun to decay. On the last leg of my voyage, I boarded a train that was so old I thought it would collapse under its own weight. As it chugged out of the station, I choked on the black soot wafting past my window and calculated six more stops before I reached my final destination. I actually got excited at the prospect, the kind of anticipation intrepid explorers must have experienced when they set foot on terra incognita for the first time, though I was bearing no gifts of wampum and disease-carrying woolen blankets, only a package of stale Mallomars.

The wheezing engine gasped its way into the station as if on life support, and I popped up to retrieve my bag from the overhead rack. The old warhorse came to a jarring halt and I lost my footing, banging my head. I quickly recovered, grabbed my wheelie-valise, and jumped onto the smoky platform where I walked toward a central reception room whose leaded-glass dome ceiling suggested faded glory. Etched metal panels were tarnished or torn away or patched over with cardboard. The still handsome sculpted mahogany cornices around the doors were scratched and in desperate need of oiling, and the fresco over the abandoned bar retained only the ghost of its original colors. In the center of the room hung a *Phantom of the Opera*–like crystal chandelier that had also seen better days. Missing glass pieces made it appear lopsided and misshapen. Half the light bulbs were blown and the remaining ones did their best, but failed to cast much of a glow. The fleur-de-lis floor tiles were cracked and faded and layered with a patina of grease, the crevices thick with grime.

Patrons were scattered about in singles and pairs facing away from each other, as still as statuary. Their oversized dark coats and parkas seemed to weigh on them, buckling their knees, bowing their legs. The sound of approaching footsteps seemed to unnerve them. They peered over their shoulders suspiciously and quickly looked away, pretending not to have heard, not to have seen.

Outside the station, teeth chattering from the penetrating cold, I waited twenty minutes for a taxi in a light sleet shower. You'd think I would have had the good sense to pack an umbrella. *Where'd you think you were going, Matt, Bermuda?* Eventually, a vehicle resembling a small hearse cranked to a halt in front of me, each of its four doors a different color, all a variation on rust.

I hopped in and said "hi" and the driver turned to me with a discomfited look on his face as if I'd surprised him during his private toilette. I thrust a piece of paper in his face. He snorted and threw the hack into gear. During the remainder of the ride, he uttered only one word, "Americanyi?" or something curiously similar. When I nodded in the affirmative, he turned and gave me the once-over, probably trying to memorize my face in case he was later questioned by the authorities.

During the progressively depressing train ride, I had tamped down my expectations of happening upon a city oozing Old World charm. But as the taxi rumbled through the perilously narrow, pitted cobblestone streets for the first time, I began to question my sanity. The town was positively Gothic and foreboding. The colorless stone or stucco and wood buildings were huddled against each other for support. The occasional architectural flourishes—floral appliqués, broken clocks, stone and tile archways—were defaced by torn flags and rotting manifestos. Metal street signs hung precariously from the sides of buildings or had long since fallen from their hinges. Only their suggestion remained.

More recent construction was of the strictly utilitarian kind, blockish and windowless. As we veered east along the banks of the frozen river, I noted several bridges of impressively ornate stone or intricate wrought iron, all in dire need of rescue. It was hard to believe that vacationers from the capital had once flocked here to sunbathe and to take in the local hot springs. Caroline had done some research and told me that dense woodlands lay just to the north and extended all the way out to the sea. She also mentioned that the burg's crown jewel was one of the oldest universities in Eastern Europe, whose delicate spires were visible through the mist. "University towns tend to be more progressive than other similarly sized or even big cities," Caroline had enthused. "Look at Austin vis-à-vis Dallas or Chapel Hill versus Charlotte."

As a going-away present, she bought me ten disposable Kodak cameras. "Soak it all up and take tons of pictures." Well, right now I was soaking all right. And shivering. Who knows what alien viruses and bacteria I had been exposed to since I left my hearth in Massapequa? A virulent cold or insidious Slavic plague was likely taking root in my system, and I wondered if they'd even heard of Robitussin in this corner of the galaxy.

I was further chagrined to discover that the right honorable Lawyer Bombyk, the man responsible for my fool's errand, was not awaiting my arrival at 222 Dreztka as agreed upon in our correspondence. I asked the cabbie to wait, flashing bills at him, but after a few minutes he started crabbing, something to the effect that I was keeping him from the thousands of fares he could be snagging in the slushy downpour—unlikely in that we hadn't passed a single, solitary human on the two-mile ride from the station.

I handed him what I'm sure was far too much money, grabbed my bags, and sought refuge under a narrow overhang that jutted from the boarded-up building adjacent to Uncle Leonard's residence. As I moved my feet in place to keep warm, I suspected that I was being spied on by a pair of stealthy eyes behind the curtains on the ground floor of 222 Dretzka. Turning my head slowly, I came face-to-face with an ancient crone whose hawk-like eyes peered through intricate lacework curtains. When I glared back at her, she defiantly held my gaze before retreating back into the darkness.

Minutes may pass like hours when you're waiting for the one you love, but they feel like weeks when you're trying to keep frostbite at bay. By and by, a thin spindle of a girl, dwarfed by a huge umbrella, appeared in the distance like a mirage and ambled slowly toward me coming to a halt about two feet away. "Matejus?"

Close enough.

While she was unlocking the front door, I ventured "And Mr. Bombyk?" She shook her head and rolled her hand in the air, the universal symbol for mañana. I followed her inside. She removed her wet raincoat and hung it on one of several hooks in the spacious downstairs hallway. She was even scrawnier without it, her low shoulders hanging down to where most of us have elbows. I shook off like a rescued barnyard animal, removed my musty-smelling overcoat, and placed it next to hers. There were double doors on one side, behind which the old lady presumably lived. I didn't have to wonder long. A piercing cackle right out of *Macbeth* arose from within. The high-pitched rant continued for a minute or so, and I wondered if she was horror-film demented or simply an aged crab venting on some other poor creature.

The young woman cocked her finger and pointed to a corkscrew staircase that was too constricting for me, my wheelie-bag, and my knapsack. "Don't bother to help. I'll make two trips," I said in a chipper voice, confident that she didn't speak sarcasm. She smiled back at me dumbly and dashed up the steps. By the time I got all my gear to the second floor landing, she had unlocked the door and offered me a large ring of keys along with a folded piece of paper. She nodded and then she was gone, pulling on her coat and opening her umbrella in one continuous motion and vanishing out the front door.

The note bore Bombyk's name, address, tomorrow's date and the words "h. 15." Because I have a master's degree, I was able to crack this arcane code: Bombyk wanted to meet the next day at his office at three p.m.

Alone at last, truly alone, for the first time since JFK Airport, I experienced that curious mixture of contentment and exhaustion you feel upon arriving at your destination in one piece, and your body signals that it's now okay to stop pumping adrenaline.

Uncle Leonard's amoeba-shaped apartment was as compact and effectively organized as the inside of an RV. Almost everything in the room was painted the same industrial white. A small skylight and a single window facing on the street kept the space from feeling claustrophobic. Just outside the disproportionately large bathroom was a draped alcove that functioned as a walk-in closet, and I'm being generous here.

One of the curved nooks in the main room housed a single bed draped with a floral chenille bedspread. The far wall was lined with shelves on which sat a teensy TV set, an old hi-fi, a short-wave radio, books, and LPs. An upholstered armchair nestled in the opposite alcove, and beside it stood a chrome reading lamp.

The block wood dining table and two chairs abutted on a wall that functioned as a kitchen with ancient appliances: a fridge with a compressor on top, a tiny four-burner from which the enamel had been rubbed away in several spots, and a shallow sink with a dripping, hook-nosed faucet in need of a new washer.

Just the sight of anything resembling a kitchen brought a rumble to my stomach, and I remembered that except for several cups of burnt coffee, I hadn't eaten since the previous evening. The fridge was empty except for a bottle of mineral water with the reassuring portrait of a contented friar on its label, some moldy cheese, and a questionable clump of dark yellow butter.

I searched through the cupboards over the sink and found an unopened box of crackers and two choices of entrée—a tin of sardines or a can of white beans. *Suck it up, kid. It's already dark out. And you're too tired to go out in search of a smart bistro in this weather.* Besides, my tootsies needed thawing, and this was the longest I'd gone without a daily shower since the last time Nathaniel and I went camping.

I'll have the beans, waiter. And what wine would you recommend with that?

As it happened, while I was foraging under the sink in search of a pot, I ran smack into a half-full bottle of Scotch, the perfect elixir for my raspy throat. So much tastier than cold medicine.

While the beans simmered, I nursed my drink as I checked out Uncle L's book and record collection: English-language editions of *Daniel Deronda* and *Herzog*, mixed in among English textbooks and foreign titles by unfamiliar authors; among the LPs were several Shostakovich concertos, the Brandenburgs, Bizet's *Pearl Fishers* and *Carmen*, *A Love Supreme*, early Louis Armstrong, Capitol-era Sinatra, some Serge Gainsbourg, and what's this, Kate Bush? Weren't you an eclectic devil, uncle?

After a not-as-hot-as-I-would-have-liked-it bath, I donned my cowboy-patterned flannel jammies and a pair of sweat socks and curled up under the chenille bedcover to enjoy my first good night's sleep since leaving Long Island.

Next morning the steely blue-gray sky had cleared, and I decided to unpack. The top dresser drawers held Uncle Leonard's shirts, sweaters, and underwear. In the closet, which gave off the faint odor of naphtha, hung several pairs of slacks, a long coat, and two suits. I transferred most of his belongings to my wheelie suitcase and stored it on the second floor landing under a skinny metal ladder that led up to the roof. I held on to a couple of his sweaters, particularly a floppy argyle cardigan I figured would be the perfect chill blocker. In the bottom dresser drawer about a half dozen black marble-faced notebooks were splayed out. After stacking them neatly, I had plenty of room for my socks and underwear. Then my stomach, tired of being ignored, struck with a sharp pang, and I went off in search of victuals.

Caroline had cautioned me not to expect one-stop shopping. Right again, old girl. Butcher, baker, dairy man, greengrocer—all with very limited selections dominated by tubers, legumes, preserved meats, and smoked fish. The bakery stocked exactly one kind of bread, the hard, crusty variety that even a great white shark would have trouble masticating. I suppose I could soak it at the bottom of a bowl of minestrone to soften it up, I thought. Now all I have to find is minestrone. They've got to have minestrone. I mean, who doesn't eat Italian food? The bakery's proprietress, a gruff potato of a woman, was in no mood for loiterers. She spewed some guttural contempt my way, words to the effect of "either buy something or get out." Don't forget, I'm from New York. I know surliness when I hear it.

The greengrocer's cupboard was similarly bare except for a selection of unwashed root vegetables, some of which Nathaniel would undoubtedly have recognized. I guessed they would come in handy if I were to make my own minestrone. Unfortunately, Nathaniel was the cook in the family, though my scrambled eggs are legendary. Then I noticed a package of dried figs, which turned out to be just as tough a chew as the bread. With every bite, I feared tearing out a filling and envisioned myself at the mercy of a local dentist, probably a circus strongman sporting a pair of bloody pliers.

The butcher was the first person to smile at me since I arrived. I decided to steer clear of the chunks of gristle on his chopping block and plunked down some local currency for a couple of meat pies, which vaguely recalled the ones my grandmother used to make. He was most obliging as I communicated with him via hand gestures. "I'll have two (peace sign), please." I held out some bills and coins and trusted him to pick out the right amount. *Oh, what I wouldn't give for the anonymity of a supermarket.*

Out on the street, I quickly downed one of the meat pies and just as quickly developed a stomachache. Small wonder. The pie was mostly hard dough with a tiny core of glutinous suet.

I arrived at exactly three p.m. in front of lawyer Bombyk's office, quite a feat considering that I had happened on his building earlier in the day only by accident. The narrow, twisty streets, whose names regularly changed, had a habit of wrapping around themselves, going east and suddenly north, then doubling back south. The law office was in a grandiose Beaux-Arts structure that loomed over a deserted square at the center of which stood a woeful statue. The heroic military figure astride the horse was smattered with decades of bird droppings and missing his right arm. The inscription on the commemorative nameplate at the base had been rubbed away.

Bombyk's place of business was a study in disproportion right out of *The Trial*. The vaulted ceiling was two stories high. An enormous two-sided clock hung down from the rafters of the cavernous central room, empty save for a tiny reception desk in the far corner and a two-person bench inside the frosted glass entry door.

Daylight filtered in through a crescent-shaped window that took up most of the wall that faced onto the square. Bombyk's assistant was not the same woman I'd met the previous day. This one had broad shoulders and blond hair that fell over one eye like Veronica Lake's. Tapping my watch, I inquired "Lawyer Bombyk?" and was met with a blank stare. Unlike those insolent Americans who try to make themselves understood by speaking English slowly and in a loud voice, I tried something a bit more sophisticated. "I have an *appuntamento*," I explained. Whatever, it seemed to do the trick. She nodded and directed me to the little bench.

In Eastern Europe, h. 15 appears to be merely an opening bid, because Bombyk, a tall, ruddy man with an aquiline nose and unruly riots of hair above each eye, didn't saunter in until just after h. 16.30, swinging his satchel as he made his way to an enclosed office at the back. Despairing, I buried my head in my hands and when I looked up again, the assistant was standing there as still as a sentinel. Suddenly gracious and solicitous, she motioned for me to follow her down the hallway to Bombyk's office, her heels tapping against the warped wooden slats.

Bombyk was studying some papers with a clear look of distaste. He smacked one of the pages with the back of his hand and grumbled, his lips curling into a semi-sneer. I took a seat in the giant wooden armchair in front of him—again, courtesy of the Kafka Collection—my feet barely touching the ground. Bombyk still didn't acknowledge me. After a few moments, he leaned back in his tiny swivel chair, fingers entwined behind his neck. Looking straight up at the ceiling he said, "Meester Robeens, how can I help to you?"

Now, I'm normally a patient man, but the warning light on my brake pads had already been flashing for over an hour. "First of all," I snarled, "you asked me to come here. And you're an hour and a half late for our appointment."

No reply.

"I'm here to discuss Leonard Baknin's estate. Does that ring a bell?"

"Ring bell?" he asked, puzzled. "What means?"

"Never mind what it means. Can we please talk about the estate?"

He sighed and reached into a pile of folders on his desk, flipped one open and, for the next hour, we discussed my inheritance. There was a bank account and a building consisting of two residential apartments and an adjacent commercial space, the one with the boarded-up front and the narrow overhang where I'd waited half-frozen the previous afternoon. I suggested selling the property, and he shook his head violently. Why not? Were market conditions unfavorable? I asked. I had learned a thing or two about real estate from Nathaniel, largely by osmosis. No, Bombyk countered. It was a most desirable property, but the purchaser would have to be amenable to allowing the old man in the downstairs apartment to remain there until he died.

"I thought an old lady lived there," I said.

"Old lady too. Not important. Just the wife." I bet Mrs. Bombyk would be so pleased.

I argued that if the couple paid rent to my uncle, they could just as easily pay the new owner. Bombyk shook his head. "Not pay rent. Live free. He many years friend your uncle."

More surprises. My uncle Leonard, it appears, was the soul of altruism, taking in strays and providing them with shelter even beyond the grave.

"What if I hang on to the property and rent out the upstairs apartment to pay for the upkeep of the building?"

Bombyk stuck a finger in one nostril and fished around. "Is possible."

"And maybe the commercial space as well," I added.

Bombyk shook his head. "Need too much work."

"Fair enough. And let's liquidate the bank account, which is how much?" Bombyk studied his notes and spoke a figure in the many hundreds of thousands, which I gathered, was local currency. In American dollars, it came out to the slightly less impressive but nonetheless tidy sum of $25,000.

"But what you do with the money?" Bombyk asked.

"Exchange it for dollars and go back home."

"No. Not possible to take so much money from country."

That stopped me dead in my tracks. Then I suggested maybe purchasing something of value like jewelry or art. Bombyk pooh-poohed the suggestion. "Very big luxury tax."

"Okay, you're the executor. You tell me."

"Spend money here. Or invest. Soviets go. Is new government. We become important," he said, dead serious.

Not to put a damper on Bombyk's nationalistic fervor, was he aware that he was talking to a severely depressed second grade teacher from Long Island who had recently attempted suicide, and not Sammy the entrepreneur from Xenia, Ohio?

"You consider," he said with a sigh, eager to get rid of me, and handed me a ream of paperwork. "Sign. Bring to me. Take time. I am here."

"I can't read any of this. It's in—"

"You must find person to translate." He shrugged as he picked up the phone and dialed. Swiveling his chair away from me toward the window, he spewed a torrent of babble into the receiver.

Chapter Four
Found in Translation

On yet another miserable morning, with the sky hovering so pendulously low you could touch it on tippy-toe, I lingered over a cup of lukewarm coffee in a blessedly overheated café. My body temperature had recently broached 101 degrees, and I was experiencing one of those dreaded "what the hell have I done?" moments. The short answer? I had left the comforts of home, wrenching myself away from anything that might remind me of Nathaniel, all in the vague hope of shocking my system out of its woeful torpor.

A moderately rational person would have opted for a sunny Greek island where he could sip ouzo and dance around and break plates. Intead, I had ventured to the world capital of institutionalized melancholia to spend the better part of each day confined to a small apartment subsisting on indigestible meat pies and listening repeatedly to Satchmo's "When It's Sleepy Time Down South." Whenever the rain or snow let up, I would swath myself in woolen scarves and two pairs of socks so my teeth didn't rattle incessantly. Then I'd wander the desolate cobblestone streets until the bottoms of my feet screamed, or I'd brave the lacerating wind blowing off the frozen river.

As I reread a three-week-old copy of *Time Magazine*'s international edition—the only English-language periodical available from the town's sole news vendor, who was located inside the central station—the words and images undulated before me. The story about some doughy former governor of Arkansas who hoped to be president struck me as completely implausible, as unlikely as my quest to find a translator for Lawyer Bombyk's estate documents.

A week earlier I had confidently marched through the corridors of the university—the town's one relatively well-preserved picturesque attraction with its medieval halls of ivy, where I tacked up neatly printed flyers: *English translator needed. Generous pay. Matthew Robins. 222 Dretzka No.2.* Thus far, the only response had been from a tentative young man with Scotch tape holding together his bottle-bottom glasses. The hapless, acne-scarred boy took one look at Bombyk's thick legal sheaf, gasped, grabbed his satchel and fled.

Heavy-eyed and dazed, I yanked myself up and walked to the café door. A steady drizzle had commenced. I was prepared. The first umbrella, a spindly portable I had purchased at a men's shop, had been carried off by a sudden gust, soaring upward toward the river embankment like a wayward kite.

My latest brolly was a sturdy British-made model boasting a handsome polished oak carved handle in the shape of a swan. With the help of a calculator I discovered among Uncle Leonard's effects, I was soon able to approximate the exchange rate. The shopkeepers, particularly the butcher, didn't appreciate my little mathematical victory, a shame since he'd been the only person who didn't glare at me as if I had just slandered him or a member of his immediate family.

Small courtesies like smiling and nodding were frowned upon in these parts. Suspicion and trepidation seemed to have become institutionalized, understandable given almost a half century of Soviet domination. And I'm sure the place wasn't exactly nirvana before that either. The citizens appeared to be wary of their neighbors, possibly even their own family members, so you can imagine their discomfort around a perfect stranger from their number one Cold War enemy. If they had experienced any sense of joy or relief at the transition from tyrannized socialist satellite to fledgling democracy, they were keeping it under their collective fur hat.

To add to the overall merriment, they had to endure regular shortages of staples like bread, eggs, and butter. On the positive side, locally distilled vodka was plentiful. The generically labeled bottle had first caught my eye on my way home from Lawyer Bombyk's. A kissing cousin to rubbing alcohol, the clear liquid provided a cheap ticket to oblivion. Since orange juice and tonic water were nowhere to be found, I drank it straight and ice cold to mask the backbite of turpentine. The ancient fridge was not good for much besides temporary storage, so I stored the bottles on the roof. The alcoholic swill took the edge off my loneliness. The price I paid was eyeball-twitching headaches in the morning.

I found my way to the central phone office at the train station and tried to call Caroline. After a couple of failed attempts, I reached her much-too-perky answering machine. I considered calling another friend, but who wants to hear "I told you so" over a scratchy transatlantic phone line? I even flirted with calling Ben, but resolved not to do so unless my persistent cough worsened into pleurisy.

On the way back to 222 Dretzka, the clouds broke and old Mr. Sun put in one of his rare appearances. I decided, cold be damned, I'm going for a jog. Maybe a good sweat will clear the toxins from my body.

As I did warm-up stretches in the hallway, my reliable downstairs gargoyle was spying on me through a crack in the double doors. *And a pleasant good afternoon to you too, lady.*

Still no sign of the alleged husband, and I wondered if perhaps he had died and she was keeping it a secret so I couldn't toss the old rattletrap out onto the street.

The streets were underpopulated as usual, mostly large delivery trucks and tradesmen. Yet from the moment I left the apartment, I had the nagging sensation that I was being followed. *Get a grip, Matt. You've been reading too many spy thrillers.*

As I raced along the promenade, I heard chunks of ice crackling on the riverbed, emitting plaintive groans as they separated into smaller floes and dashed against the abutment. The trees, weary of hibernation, were tentatively shaking off winter with the vague promise of sprouts. As I stopped for a moment to heave some phlegm into one of Uncle Leonard's monogrammed linen handkerchiefs, a pitiful little motorbike buzzed past, pulled a sharp U-turn, and strafed me a second time.

The driver, an androgynous, possibly female, slab of beef in a punk leather jacket and a Buster Brown hairdo sized me up with a wicked grin. Since there wasn't a soul within shouting distance, I assumed a mugging was afoot. *Oh, did you hear? Matt got beat up and robbed by a fat chick on a moped during his Eastern European trip.* A small three-wheeler delivery truck putt-putted past me, and I tried in vain to flag it down. Undeterred, Little Miss Hell's Angel circled me several times, like a spider spinning out its web.

Screeching to a halt in front of me, motor still purring, she said in a loud voice, "You are Matthew, yes?" I nodded. "I am Olga. I be your translator."

"Well, why didn't you say so in the first place?" I said. "I thought you were trying to rob me."

She tossed back her head and laughed. "This is not U.S. Such things here…almost never."

On the way back to the apartment, I asked how she knew who I was. "You doing the running, and in the winter," she said with a sardonic chuckle, as if such behavior was reserved for the demented. "And you wear the Nikes." My athletic shoes, she informed me, were as rare and prized as Fabergé eggs. If I was willing to part with them or a pair of my trusty 501s she promised to get me "very good price."

Olga propped her dinky, battered bike against the boarded-up storefront next to 222. "Are you sure it will be safe there?" I asked.

Again, she scoffed. "This piece of shit? I have to pay them to steal it." She grabbed her backpack and barreled past me into the hallway. The old lady threw open the double doors, affording me my first clear look at her—a screaming meanie right out of a Grimm fairy tale complete with a bun of frizzy hair and a gargantuan mole on her left cheek. She began spitting vituperations at Olga, who gave as good as she got. As the row escalated, I was distracted by the sight of a dazed, obviously hard-of-hearing old man sitting in a wheelchair. He was stooped over like a question mark, staring into space as if he was desperately trying to remember something simple like his own name, but it stubbornly eluded him.

Olga finally shouted the old woman down and, with a low, deflated rumble, she retreated back into her lair and snapped the doors tightly shut.

"What was that all about?"

"She think I am prostitute. I tell her, 'You miserable peasant, I am university student,' and she must go to fuck herself."

"I think I'm in love with you." I laughed and coughed up something productive into my handkerchief.

Any doubts I may have entertained about Olga's translating skills were immediately quashed when she whipped out a tattered English-language legal dictionary. "We have good law school at university," she explained. "But is one thing I must ask. Do you want every word or big idea?"

"Big idea? Oh, you mean paraphrase?"

I could tell I'd lost her. As I explained, she nodded and smiled. "I like this word—para-phrase."

I assured her that a blow-by-blow wasn't necessary, but I certainly needed to grasp all the salient points, especially my legal rights and obligations concerning the estate. We agreed on a pay schedule and quickly developed a shorthand communication. If she understood what I'd just said, she would nod. If she leaned forward and her eyes narrowed in confusion, I knew to backtrack and clarify. Over the next three hours, sustained by tea and crackers with jam, we made substantial progress.

"Let's take a break now. It's already dark and your family must be expecting you home for dinner," I said.

She shrugged. "Is always dark in the winter. At home, only my brother and me. And he go to another town for to do working. My mother is under the ground and my father, I think he live in Germany."

"In that case, how would you like to join me for dinner? My treat."

"I say yes."

"And I say great. Just let me change my shirt. I want you to take me to your favorite restaurant. Price is no object."

Café au Poivre was French in name only, more of a roadhouse than a bistro, the menu consisting of the standard potages and goulashes tarted up with French names. "What do you like here?" I asked.

"The beef stew. You please to order for me," she whispered as a supremely disinterested waitress neared.

"But I don't speak the language." Olga shook her head

and disappeared behind the menu. I pointed out our selections to the waitress, a wispy-looking young woman with an "I'm so friggin' bored I could die" pout. After she returned to the kitchen, Olga put down the menu and I noticed that her cocky façade had fallen away and she was suddenly as defenseless and adorable as Darla in *The Little Rascals*.

Warmed by a few swigs of dark alc, I flung off my coat and draped it over the back of my chair. When I turned back, Olga's eyes widened and she was again all piss and vinegar, clapping her hands in delight and rocking in her seat.

"But this is wonderful. You are a gay." She laughed. "And a Jew. And an American. This is the first time I meet someone like that."

"Which one?"

"All of them." Olga explained that Americans rarely ventured to this neck of the woods, that there were only a smattering of Jews in town, and the only gays she knew were the over-the-top-can't-miss-'em variety from school. And here I was, a veritable trifecta.

"I'm curious. What tipped you off that I was gay?"

She pointed to my T-shirt.

"You know what Silence = Death means?"

Olga rolled her eyes. Leaning across the table she whispered, "It is from the Act Up. I know this because I too am a gay."

"Lesbian," I corrected her just as the waitress returned with our entrees and plopped them down in front of us. Olga turned several shades of red and bolted from the table. The waitress scowled as if she'd had run off without paying the tab.

I was at a loss for what had just happened. Just when you think you're getting the hang of the locals, they pull something weird like that. But hey, I wasn't complaining. I'd only been here for a couple of weeks, and I already had my own personal lesbian. Some people claim that the term "gaydar" simply means the ability to pick out fellow travelers in a crowd, but I believe that it's also a homing mechanism, a dog whistle only those of a similar affection can hear.

Olga returned a few minutes later and, without a word of explanation, began shoveling food down her gullet.

"I'm sorry. Did I say something wrong?" I asked, guilt being my normal fallback position. She ignored me and continued chowing down. When she was done, she pushed the plate away and eyed me closely. "Matthew. You have the AIDS?"

She caught me mid-bite and after I finished gagging, I said, "No, as in negative."

"Because why?" she asked.

"Because I only had one partner for years."

"He is where?"

"He passed away recently."

"Ah. I understand now why you have the unhappy face. He have the AIDS?"

"No, why do you keep asking that?"

"Do not all the American gays have the AIDS?"

"No, it only seems that way sometimes."

"Then why you wear this shirt?"

"Solidarity. I'm sure you know what that means. Now it's my turn. Are you out? Do you have a girlfriend?"

Olga clasped her heart and, again, the tough-girl façade vanished, and she was once again a round-faced Kewpie doll bravely trying to contain her swelling emotions.

"No. I am virgin." (with a W, how adorable is that?)

"Then how do you know you're a lesbian?"

Olga pursed her lips and lowered her eyes to half mast.

"I withdraw the question."

The waitress approached with the check and when Olga turned away sharply, even dumb old me finally caught on.

"So that's it. You have the hots for the surly waitress."

"What is hots?"

I rapidly tapped my palm against my heart and cocked my head in the waitress's direction.

Olga blushed deep crimson. "Everybody can see this? I will die."

"So is she interested?"

Olga shrugged and shook her head.

"How do you know? Have you spoken to her?"

"Just to order the food. I am afraid."

"Well, I grant you, she is a bit on the unapproachable side," I said, turning to take a good look in case I'd overlooked some hidden charm.

"No. Nina is goddess."

"Oh, so now it's Nina, siren of the Nile, mistress of desire."

"She very nice when *he* not here." Olga twitched her right shoulder toward the far wall where, huddled over a large bowl of borscht under a discolored Toulouse-Lautrec poster of La Goulue, sat a lumbering oaf in a salt-and-pepper woolen trench with a black scarf wrapped around his neck like a tenor safeguarding his vocal cords.

"Ralf," she said and for a second I thought she'd barked. "They are promised," she sighed.

"Then she clearly plays for the other team and you need to move on."

"No. Is Nina or no one. I cannot sleep. I cannot eat." This despite her impersonation of a starving orphan not ten minutes earlier.

"We all get unrequited crushes, dear. They pass."

After I explained the word "unrequited," she protested, "No. Is Nina and only Nina."

"Except Nina is marrying Ralf."

Olga puffed her cheeks and expelled a defeated gust of air. "In three months."

"Exactly."

"You are correct. I must say something to her. But I choke when I try to talk," she said, which touched even my mothballed heart. "We go. I cannot be here."

When I approached Nina to settle accounts, she went from blasé to hostile, baring her fangs. She tossed the change at me, heavy coins flying helter and skelter. No tip for you, young lady, I thought, as I bent over and when I got up, I noticed her staring at Olga as she walked out the door.

Hmmm. I wonder…

I rushed outside and before the door was completely closed, swept Olga into my arms and tried to plant a kiss. She immediately pushed me away. "Stop. What you doing?"

"Just an experiment," I whispered and peered through the front window at Nina. *If looks could kill…*

So, sullen Nina was perhaps not completely indifferent to Olga, I thought, marveling at the inscrutability of sexual attraction. Since there's nothing better than some philanthropic work to snap one out of a deep funk, I resolved that my new mission was to bring these two love-starved damsels together.

Over the next several days, after knocking off from our translating work, Olga and I either dined at Café au Poivre together or I sent her on alone, claiming a headache or lack of appetite. Each time we arrived as a couple, Nina was distant and surly, and I assumed she was spitting in my beef stew. Well, to actually call it beef stew would be hyperbolic. Soupçon of beef stew was more like it. When Olga went on her own, however, Nina was chatty and tried to draw her out, asking personal questions about her family and life at the university, all of it leading up to the twenty-four-thousand-dollar question: "Who's the American bozo, and what is he to you?"

I'm happy to report that my little scheme quickly bore fruit. One night, just as I was just drifting off to sleep, there was a sledgehammer knock at the front door. I peered out the window and there stood Olga gesticulating wildly and pleading to be let in.

"She love me," were her first words as she danced through the door, then without pause, burst into tears. "I am so unhappy."

"Calm down. Let's have a shot of vodka, and then you can fill me in on all the details."

To paraphrase Eliza Doolittle, "vodka was mother's milk to her." Olga had been drinking the stuff since she was in diapers. Fortunately, she was not a sloppy or an angry drunk, but the kind who turns reflective and philosophical. After three generous tumblers of clear gold, she spilled: During dinner, Nina had pummeled her with questions about "the Yankee dog" (yes, Mr. Gorbachev, that's the thanks we get for helping tear down that wall). When, per my coaching, Olga played it cool, hinting that she and I might be playing hide the liverwurst, Nina reprimanded her. I was all wrong for Olga; it could only lead to heartbreak. Olga then deftly turned the tables. Since they were on the subject of ill-suited boyfriends, why was she engaged to that lump Ralf, who always sat in the corner with that preposterous scarf wrapped around his neck, noisily lapping up borscht, and never uttered a single kind word to her?

"That's my girl," I chimed. "So what did she say?"

Olga's bluntness knocked the wind out of Nina's sails, and she collapsed into a chair. The sight of her angel in distress unnerved Olga. Unable to still her tongue any longer, she professed undying love.

"I swear on the saints, I do not know I am going to say it. It jump from my mouth," she said. Being something of a faux-pas expert myself, I didn't doubt her for a minute; although, to be honest, deep down we all know there really are no accidents.

Once Nina had recovered from shock, she admitted to similar stirrings for Olga. Then they both had a good cry, after which they retreated to the alley behind the restaurant and made out until their lips were sore.

"This is fantastic," I said, quite proud of myself. "So why the long face?"

"Because Nina tell me she must still marry Ralf," Olga said mid-sob. "My life is finished."

Chapter Five
Black & White Marble

Awarning to aspiring matchmakers everywhere: den-mothering a lovesick teenage motorcycle mama is a tedious and ultimately thankless job. Olga's moods ping-ponged from giddy to morbid, often in the span of a single day. Nina loves me, she loves me not. Nina loves me, but she's still going to marry that lout Ralf and bear his children. I am the luckiest person in the world/I wish I'd never been born. Honestly, who'da thunk a butch dyke could be so girly?

A lesbian soap opera, however, was exactly the kind of "queer-life-goes-on" diversion I needed to shift focus from my own sorry melancholic state. My leave of absence from school extended only through September, when I would have to return to "real life" in that big, empty house. For the present, I occupied myself with the impending settlement of Uncle Leonard's estate and all the clever ways I could spend the inheritance money, since I wasn't allowed to take more than the equivalent of a thousand American dollars out of the country at a time. A vintage Longines Luftwaffe wristwatch jumped out at me like a wicked temptress when I passed a jeweler's window downtown. Even though it was Swiss-made, I couldn't get past the fact that it commemorated the German air force. If I bought it, would my face melt like the Nazi villain in *Raiders of the Lost Ark*?

On the plus side, now that Nina was hip to my efforts in bringing her and Olga together, she found me downright tolerable. She even kissed me on the cheek one afternoon to thank me for lending them the apartment for the official de-flowering. The rafters shook and the heavens opened up or so they claimed, far more than I cared to know.

On the evenings Nina worked late, I had Olga pretty much to myself, and we attended the recently instituted film series at the university. In a gesture of freedom and magnanimity, the new democratically elected central government had recently lifted the decades-long Soviet ban on any movie that didn't toe the socialist line, which pretty much included any film made in the West over the past forty years.

The dated campus theater boasted butt-numbing wooden seats and a sound system with all the clarity of a short-wave radio transmission from Antarctica. The audience had started out small, but as word spread, the crowds doubled from week to week until the theater could no longer accommodate the swell of students and townspeople starved for entertainment and an approximation of what had transpired in the outside world during their enforced absence. Little things like the sexual revolution.

The film series moved to the school auditorium with its similarly uncomfortable metal fold-out chairs, seat cushions having yet to reach the Eastern bloc. Regardless, the audience had few complaints and latecomers were content to sit in the aisles or outside the auditorium's double doors. Since our arrival time depended on Olga's fluctuating romantic barometer, I often found myself literally out in the cold watching my favorite movies by Truffaut, Hitchcock, Fellini, Antonioni, Kurosawa, Ford, and Bergman on a forty-five degree angle. Not much of a hardship since I could recite some of them by heart and was more interested to see how the audiences received them on first viewing. None of them seemed to mind that most of the 16 mm prints were scratchy and often neither dubbed nor subtitled; they devoured the movies whole.

Depending on the film, the screenings sometimes took on the tenor of a revival meeting. Each movie was treated as a revelation, and between reel changes, the viewers argued about what they'd seen as if they were parsing passages of the Torah. The few polyglots in the group, Olga included, updated the others on plot nuances, and I became the go-to person about American life as it was portrayed. The passionate debates continued long after the end credits. School officials had to threaten everything short of incarceration to persuade the audience members to go home.

La Dolce Vita, which to most of the Western world was already a period piece, practically caused a riot, sharply dividing viewers between those who deemed it a brilliant satire on Western decadence and others who labeled it soft-core porn. Nonetheless, the ladies fanned themselves every time Marcello Mastroianni waltzed across the screen and the men were no less discombobulated by the sight of the buxom Anita Ekberg. But the reaction was positively muted compared to the night *Psycho* was screened. During the infamous shower scene, about a half dozen viewers ran screaming from the room as if being pursued by the hounds of hell, and afterward, the film prompted a diatribe on the evils of capitalism. The Janet Leigh character's provocative liaison with John Gavin in the opening scene and her brazen theft of bank funds deposited by the proletariat was proffered as sufficient justification for her grisly murder. The Soviets were gone, but their peculiar worldview on the corrupting effect of Western culture and suitable retribution persisted.

Olga was over the moon about this expansive view beyond her borders and it was a relief to have something to discuss with her that concerned neither the estate papers nor Nina, Nina, Nina. Who was this Cary Grant (*North by Northwest*) for whom she swore she would throw over even her one true love? Why did John Wayne (*The Searchers*) walk so funny and talk out of the side of his mouth like a drunkard? How could anyone conjure a world as magical and triste as *Juliet of the Spirits*? And what did this idiot Godard (*La Chinoise*) know about Marxism? "I would like to invite him to spend some time living in a Communist state. Then we shall see if he feels the same," she sneered. Nathaniel would have *so* approved.

Another film that captured her fancy was Howard Hawks's *Ball of Fire*. Quite apart from a massive crush she developed on Barbara Stanwyk, she was tickled by the witty dissection of '40s slang such as hep cat and daddy-o. Most of the words were archaic and defied precise translation, but I did my best. I told her that almost all American slang from the Jazz Era on originated with African Americans, which she found particularly fascinating since she had also never met a person of color. I guaranteed her that she'd forget all about Cary Grant when the university scheduled any film starring Sidney Poitier. *I'll call you Mr. Tibbs anytime you like, Sidney.*

At school Olga had been taught the "Queen's English," not its American country cousin. So in addition to slang, whenever a colorful idiom haphazardly fell from my lips like "you're bringing me down" and "like a hole in the head," her face would go dead and she'd lean forward. "What it means, 'I bring you down'?" When I explained, she would laugh appreciatively and write down these precious *bon mots*. Occasionally, she'd try them out on me and invariably get them delightfully wrong.

The estate documents finally signed and notarized,

Bombyk promised to transfer the assets as quickly as possible which, by this time, I realized meant "don't pack your bags just yet." While looking for somewhere to stash my copy of the voluminous document, I again stumbled across the marbleized notebooks in the bottom drawer of Uncle Leonard's dresser. I showed one to Olga, as much out of curiosity as to change the subject during one of her ceaseless conversations about Nina. We had just returned from a screening of Truffaut's *Jules and Jim,* and she was reconfiguring the story with her, Nina, and Ralf as the three main characters. I shipped her off with a couple of the notebooks under her arm. She promised to take a look and report back anything of interest.

The temperature outdoors was warming up a bit but still as bracing as a crisp fall afternoon back home, which made me think of football, which made me think of Nathaniel, which led to a crying jag. These days my weep-athons had musical accompaniment, Uncle Leonard's recording of Bizet's *The Pearl Fishers*, containing the ultimate male bonding duet, "Au Fond du Temple Saint." After the first few notes, I was a complete wreck.

My appreciation for the duet, however, was not always shared by my downstairs neighbors. When I brought the stylus back to the start for a second or third playing—once was never enough—Frau Killjoy began pounding on the ceiling with her broom. I responded with some foot banging and then ran downstairs and rapped loudly on her door, fully prepared to give her a piece of what was left of my mind. She came at me guns blazing, pointing to her husband, who was keening as if he was reciting Kaddish, and blamed me for his distress. So I took pity on the poor schmo, turned off the hi-fi, got into bed, wrestled with insomnia, and lost. At two in the morning I pulled on my running gear and jogged myself into exhaustion. When I walked in the door, I was startled to find Olga sitting in the dark in an armchair like the bad guy in a detective story.

"Where you been?" she squealed, holding up one of the notebooks. "This, my friend, is dynamite shit."

Olga was not whistlin' Dixie.

NOTEBOOK ONE (1936)

The one boy is named Tonio, the other Isaac.

They have been friends since the day they met in middle school. Isaac is the better student and tutors his friend in the afternoons to prepare him for final exams. In athletics, however, it is Tonio who excels. Though Isaac tries his best, he can barely keep up with Tonio and the other teammates on the soccer field, the running track, and particularly at rowing. Tonio patiently encourages his friend and is quick to come to his defense when the others, as young men sometimes do, chide or demean Isaac for missing a pass on the field or because of his poor skills as an oarsman. Tonio slyly deflects the criticism by pointing to their inadequacies, which immediately silences his cohorts. He is sufficiently respected and well-liked that they do not dare accuse him of favoritism or partiality.

Tonio is aware that their disparagements are, in part, envy of Isaac's superior scholarship, which they hold up as confirmation of his otherness. For all his friend's encouragement, however, Isaac has no illusion that he will ever be more than an average athlete. He is neither gifted nor sufficiently driven to overcome his mediocrity. But what he lacks in talent, he tries to compensate for with dedication. Tonio admires his pluck and is quick to offer constructive suggestions as to how he might improve.

Today is Sunday. Their coach has granted the players a rare day of rest. But, at Isaac's urging, Tonio has agreed to spend a few hours trying to improve his rowing technique. Tonio has repeatedly assured him that, while he is not as adept as the others, he nonetheless makes a fair contribution to the crew. Even their coach has begrudgingly admitted as much, and Tonio reminds Isaac that he is not a man to casually dispense praise. Still, Isaac is dissatisfied. As always, he is his own worst critic. He cannot understand why his arms and shoulders are not yet strong despite the daily weight-training regimen Tonio mapped out for him, and which he has followed to the letter. He also becomes frustrated when he gets winded easily and, on occasion, cramps up. It is merely a question of correcting his posture and continuing to build the muscles in his upper body, Tonio assures him. Don't give up hope, Isaac. You must believe in yourself as I do.

Today they plan to concentrate on the posture problems and ways to apportion his energy more efficiently. As team captain, Tonio has a set of keys to the boathouse. He and Isaac retrieve a small rowboat and carry it above their heads to the wharf where they carefully lower it into the water. Isaac gets in first and Tonio passes him the oars and two towels. They set out onto the river, slowly warming up to ensure that Isaac's muscles don't cramp when they reach full rowing speed. As always, Isaac is anxious to court Tonio's favor. After all, it is only natural for a young man to desire his closest friend's good opinion, he tells himself.

With his other teammates, Tonio can be quite a taskmaster, but with Isaac, he is patient and supportive. He suspects that the real reason for Tonio's deference is his gratitude for Isaac's tutoring, without which Tonio would fall hopelessly behind in his schoolwork. Isaac can be demanding of Tonio, though he is less forthcoming with words of praise of encouragement. Even when he admires Tonio's efforts, he is simply incapable of doling out compliments without sounding false, and Tonio would surely see through that. It is a matter of temperament. Tonio is naturally affable and popular. Isaac is a more interior person, less convivial, and his attempts at flattery often sound hollow.

This Sunday begins as a warm and especially sunny fall day. As the morning progresses, however, a large bank of dense clouds gathers in the far corner of the sky. The wind picks up, and the thick clouds soon obscure the sun. The scent of imminent rainfall permeates the air. Tonio's mood seems to darken with the clouds. He rides Isaac especially hard, bluntly criticizing him, which only eats away at his friend's already fragile confidence. Isaac prays for a kind word or a small pat on the back to acknowledge that, even if he has fallen short, Tonio understands that he is giving his all. Without Tonio's reassurances, he fears that he will succumb to the growing soreness in his muscles.

But Tonio only grows more rigid and dismissive as the morning progresses. As any chance of impressing his friend fades, Isaac becomes distressed. His breathing turns shallow and the pain in his shoulder becomes almost unbearable.

Why are you deliberately ignoring what I tell you? Tonio yells after again correcting Isaac's posture. I don't know why I gave up my Sunday to come out here. You are hopeless, utterly hopeless.

As the first drops of rain begin to fall, Tonio turns away from Isaac as if repulsed by the sight of him.

Stung, as if by a scorpion, Isaac's shoulder spasms, and one of the oars slips from his grasp and glides away. Get it, Tonio shouts. When Isaac hesitates, he tosses him from the boat, forbidding him to return without the oar even if he has to swim all the way downriver to retrieve it. Isaac dutifully goes off in pursuit, fighting against the gelid water temperature and the paralyzing cramps. Tonio regards him with what can only be characterized as disdain. He is probably thinking *I am right to demand more of him.*

The sky, now a solid gray, opens up just as Isaac returns with the wayward oar, and Tonio pulls him into the boat. They both wonder if they can make it upstream to the boathouse before taking on too much water. Tonio points to a barn on the opposite embankment, which Isaac can barely make out through the steady stream of rainwater. Quickly, Tonio says, we must reach the other side. Give me your best effort this time. Do not disappoint me again.

Drenched and downtrodden, Isaac makes a sincere effort to match his friend's powerful strokes biting down on his tongue to distract himself from the pain. By the time they reach the riverbank, it is pouring. They flip the boat over their heads and take cover in the barn, leaning against the doorway out of breath, panting and shaking themselves off like drenched dogs. They gaze silently at the downpour and, occasionally, at one another, attempting to gauge the other's mood. Neither wants to be the first to speak, which is strange since they usually never have the slightest problem with conversation. There is rarely a thought or insight they are not eager to share with one other. They are often amazed at how much in agreement they are on virtually every subject and how quickly time passes when they are in each other's company.

Isaac's jersey is fused to his skin and, because of his sore shoulder, he is having great difficulty removing it. Tonio comes up behind him and helps peel the shirt over Isaac's head. Isaac returns the favor. When Isaac starts to shiver uncontrollably, Tonio, who is still standing behind him, also begins to tremble, as if in sympathy. Isaac turns to face him and both appear frightened, yet neither can break the other's gaze.

Tonio speaks first. Does this have to be? he asks. Isaac is aware that if he says no that will be the end of it and the subject will never come up again. But he cannot bring himself to utter the word. He places his palm against the nape of Tonio's neck and soothingly caresses it.

NOTEBOOK TWO (1939)

Since entering university, Isaac and Tonio's fortunes have shifted. Tonio has blossomed as a student, while Isaac, distracted by political upheaval and family troubles, has faltered. Isaac's father, Meyer, a respected bank manager, has recently been relieved of his position. No specific reason was given. His superior, a kindly gentleman, was clearly uncomfortable with the decision and discreetly slipped Meyer a generous severance—which he was specifically forbidden to do—exacting a solemn promise that he make no mention of it, not even to his family.

Meanwhile, Tonio's father, Edvard, once a lowly government clerk, quite suddenly has been promoted to a position of prominence in the local government and is now paid deference by the same neighbors who previously regarded him as a man lacking substance. Edvard is flattered by the newfound attention. But ever mindful that the winds could easily shift against him at any time, he takes great pains to ensure his family is not tainted by even the slightest hint of impropriety.

One of the first casualties is his son's friendship with Isaac who, until now, has paid almost daily visits to their home. Edvard informs Tonio that it is time for him to expand his circle of acquaintances. He says it in a good-natured way to be sure. That is the only way to persuade Tonio, who can be quite stubborn, particularly when it comes to Isaac. His son is too good-hearted, Edvard reasons. But the time for boyhood friendships is past, and he needs to be more careful with whom he associates. Besides, he should be focusing on his future, selecting a suitable profession and making the acquaintance of a young lady for a favorable marriage and the perpetuation of the family name.

Isaac and Tonio's clandestine meetings now must be even more carefully planned. In summer, they usually take separate seaside vacations and yet somehow end up staying at the same obscure hotel in the same remote fishing village where they are certain not to be recognized, though they take the extra precaution of arriving and departing on different days.

Their fall hunting trips, however, have been canceled. Tonio is too well known locally, as much due to his popularity as a student and sportsman as for being the son of a prominent city official, the recently elected mayor's right-hand man. Even at school, Tonio and Isaac now speak only if they happen to be in the same class. Tonio pretends not to notice that his other classmates deliberately snub Isaac, though if one of them is so brazen enough to voice his distaste, he cows the young man into silence.

For a time, despite the increasing likelihood of war, Tonio and Isaac manage to continue their trysts, which are now tinged with unspoken melancholy. Finally, the day arrives when the inevitable can no longer be forestalled. On this day, like St. Peter, Tonio will deny Isaac three times and they will be separated, perhaps forever. The night before, at that same abandoned barn several miles downriver where they had taken refuge on that gloomy, marvelous Sunday, Tonio confesses to Isaac that unless they are close enough to breathe the same air, then it is not worth breathing. Isaac, always the more pragmatic of the two, does what he can to reassure Tonio that their separation will be temporary, making promises not even he believes he can keep.

The next morning, at a meeting of students and teachers in the assembly hall, the proctor urges the expulsion of certain undesirables at the school, effective immediately. Tonio is among the first to raise his voice in agreement. He has been ordered to do so by his father, who advised him of the decision in advance, and who Tonio believes was one of its fiercest proponents. Be enthusiastic in your support, Edvard urged his son. The others will follow your example. And truly, his solidarity with the proctor carries great weight with the few wavering professors and students.

Isaac and others from his part of town are

conspicuously absent from the convocation. In recent months, some of the young men and women he grew up with have moved away, a few with their families. These increasingly common departures are rarely remarked upon anymore, except for wishes of safe passage.

Tonio's second rebuff occurs along the city's main thoroughfare. Isaac, on an errand for his mother, is at the curb when Tonio's family car, a handsome roadster with a running board, stops for a traffic signal. Edvard is at the wheel staring straight ahead, and Tonio is in the backseat beside his mother looking out the window. Isaac calls out to him and waves. At that precise moment, Tonio turns his head sharply and pretends to engage his mother in conversation.

Later that afternoon, Tonio and his new girlfriend, Alysha, are enjoying themselves with other schoolmates at a tavern near the outskirts of the city. The ale house is one enormous room with an arched ceiling in which even the softest word is amplified. Today's discussion is particularly heated, the topic being the morning's assembly and the almost unanimous consensus to expel the undesirables.

Boris, one of the larger and more obstreperous lads, challenges Tonio. He is surprised, he says, that Tonio was so amenable, especially since everyone knows the Jew, Isaac, is among his closest friends. Tonio dismisses his assertion. You're exaggerating, Bruno. Isaac is merely a childhood acquaintance, hardly what one would call a dear friend, he says. Boris, the worse for alcohol, continues to goad him, hoping to get a rise out of Tonio and perhaps bring him down a peg.

When Alysha comes to Tonio's defense, Boris teases him mercilessly for hiding behind a woman's skirt. Tonio assures Boris he is well capable of defending himself. His voice rising with each word, he asserts that if he once took pity and befriended Isaac, it was out of naïveté, before he fully understood the true perfidy of his race. Should Isaac walk into the tavern at this very moment, Tonio proclaims, he would spit in his face and bloody him. Cheers and gales of laughter rise from the table and echo through the tavern.

Because his comrades are so immersed in their cruel jibes, only Tonio notices that Isaac has been sitting way in the back the entire time and is now quietly exiting, valise in hand. Isaac glances back at him only for a second and with no particular expression on his face. But Tonio is seized by a giant wave of nausea and feels a sudden need to vomit. Bruno is delighted by Tonio's loss of composure. It is good to see you are not above a good puke now and then like the rest of us, he laughs, pleased to be the source of Tonio's discomfort.

By nightfall, Isaac has walked several miles and is passing through a small town when Tonio's family car drives past. He pretends not to notice. An hour later, on a lonely stretch of road, Isaac sees the car again, parked on a shoulder. He walks around to the passenger side and climbs in.

Tonio and Isaac are together for the last time and afterward they drive all night to the sea, where a fisherman they befriended during one of their summer visits awaits them.

They have already said their good-byes. Though they are aware they may never see each other again, they try to be stoic, having already shed too many tears in private. They have time for one last fraternal hug and then Isaac boards the vessel. Tonio stands on the wharf and watches as the motorboat moves out to sea. He remains there until the boat is absorbed by the darkness. Isaac does not look back, not even once, fearing that if he does, he will throw himself overboard.

Tonio returns home. He is prepared to suffer the consequences of his father's ire when, after dressing for work, Edvard notices his car is missing. Isaac helped him construct the perfect alibi. He was drunk, he will tell his father, and when Alysha, his virtuous lady friend, refused his advances, he took refuge at the local brothel. His father will pretend to be angry for appearances' sake.

The next evening, as Isaac boards a trawler bound for North America and is asked for his passport and identity papers, he has already ceased to be himself. His dark hair is now several shades lighter and combed forward just like Tonio's, whose identity he has assumed. There is no particular resemblance between them except for the hair color, Tonio's wire-rimmed spectacles, and a diamond-patterned shirt, the same one his friend is wearing in his passport photo. What enables Isaac to embody his friend is something more subtle, which not even he can fully appreciate. Over the many years they have spent in each other's company, Isaac and Tonio have unconsciously appropriated each other's facial expressions and gestures. It is not uncommon for dear friends and married couples to appropriate the speech patterns and mannerisms of their intimates. The melding of identities is a testament to their affection.

Isaac is impressed by the ease with which he is accepted as Tonio by every official he encounters on his journey through Canada and the United States, where he arrives unannounced at his sister's doorstep in New York. In planning his departure, his family had decided that Isaac needed to vanish without a trace. Not even his sister was to know of it, since his father suspected that the family's movements and conversations were being monitored by the authorities.

Several months later, when it is discovered that Tonio's passport and identification papers are missing, he feigns surprise. He must have lost them during his summer vacation, he tells his father. He had taken his passport along because he was planning a side trip to Scandinavia, but he changed his mind at the last minute. Edvard pretends to believe him, though he has guessed the truth. His son has been duped by an unscrupulous young man under the guise of friendship. That person is long gone, so the unfortunate incident need never come to light. He will see to it that Tonio is quickly issued new identity papers, though it is of little consequence. War has recently been declared and Tonio will soon enlist in the local military regiment. As the eldest son of an important government official, Tonio must lead by example.

CHAPTER SIX
SPRING IS HERE (I HEAR)

Translating the first two notebooks into semi-intelligible English was quite a task. Olga and I were at it well into the morning. First she would provide me with a rough précis of each sentence. Then we'd flip around verbs, nouns, and modifiers until it cohered into plausible, if in no way elegant, English. In the excitement, Olga missed her first class of the day and had to rush to make second period. After she left, I collapsed into a semi-coma, my physical energy sapped, my mind swimming as I tried to digest the new information.

Were Uncle Leonard's notebooks thinly veiled auto-biography, or was he merely fantasizing a love affair with some childhood friend? Or perhaps the characters were entirely fictional and the story represented a sexually repressed young man's plaintive yearning for romantic connection. What really floored me was that just as I had convinced myself that the trip to Eastern Europe was not preordained, good old Uncle Leonard pitched me a curve ball. Though he hadn't a clue of my existence, much less our affectional similarities, he had reached out through time and space and directed me to the bottom drawer of his dresser. Think about it. Almost anyone else who'd found the notebooks would probably have tossed them unread. I almost did. I wondered how often throughout history, other such revelatory documents have been accidentally discarded and how different our understanding of the past might be if more of them had come to light.

The lives of the two young lovers filtered through my half-dormant brain, prompting a series of unsettling dreams about which I remember very little except for some S.S. types straight chasing me through the streets of town, my brother Ben among them. When I woke up mid-afternoon, I lingered in bed for a while, trying to recall what Auntie Edna had told me about Leonard's years in America. If the information in the notebooks was even remotely true, it would explain his haste to return home right after the war and why, after learning his family's fate, he chose to remain even in the face of crushing Soviet oppression. The romantic in me wanted to believe that Isaac and Tonio had existed in real life. Even if my uncle and his secret lover hadn't actually been intimate, perhaps the man he called "Tonio" had put himself on the line for Leonard and helped him escape. And if that isn't love...

Whatever new revelations were contained in the remaining books would have to wait. What with all her work on the estate papers and her blossoming romance with Nina, Olga had been neglecting her schoolwork. Nina and I promised to take a step back to give her time to cram for finals.

Another unforeseen consequence of my discovery: The tale of the ill-fated young lovers stoked my dampened libidinal fires. After several months of sexual apathy bordering on distaste, I'd come to accept celibacy. Having been at the mercy of my urges since the age of twelve, the respite, though involuntary, was not entirely unwelcome.

Now, like someone suffering from a prolonged loss of appetite, I was suddenly ravenous, stimulated by everything from the warm water in my bath to the softness of the worn cotton sheets, to the sticky sweet aroma of apple and plum cakes at the local bakery. My inner satyr awakened, self-pleasure would not begin to satisfy my needs. What I craved was a lusty, unfettered, pulse-pounding, delirium-inducing *folie à deux*.

And not to put too fine a point on it, spring was here at last. Clusters of colorful crocus, abelia, bluebells, and anemones poked through the surface of the dormant, frozen ground, flourishing in windowsills and in the flower beds lining the squares and local parks. Sparrows and finches and larks proudly announced their return from rooftops and treetops. The once-sparse streets were suddenly thronged with men walking to work, whistling and doffing their hats at young mothers pushing prams and softly cooing at their babies. Young lovers ambled arm in arm along the river bridges, their eyes moist with attraction, or loitered on the benches lining the promenade waving as I jogged by.

And I was no longer the sole runner. Other lads kept pace with me, gleaming with sweat, breathing heavily and exuding a fatal musk that made my head dance. If I didn't find someone to cool my spring fever, I was convinced I would die from it, like an unrequited lover from an eighteenth-century novel who wastes away after the object of his desire takes the veil and retreats to a cloister. *"He perished from unslaked passion,"* the *doctor sighed as he drew the tear-soaked linen sheet over the young man's pallid face.*

Back in the Big Apple, I would have had no trouble finding a willing partner for an evening of face sucking and body slamming. But in a country where being gay had been decriminalized about five minutes ago, and the closet was still firmly shut, I hadn't the vaguest idea where to turn. Olga was currently neck deep in her studies, so the only other sympathetic ear I could bend was Nina's.

I discovered that beneath her reserved exterior beat the heart of a true fatalist. She was the perfect antidote to Olga's pie-in-the-sky take on life. While the latter viewed obstacles as a personal affront, Nina was from the "if life gives you lemons" school. Nowhere was this more apparent than in her attitude toward her fiancé. While Olga wanted to will him out of existence, Nina was resigned to the arrangement, accepting it as one would a congenital defect that she refused to let compromise her goals. She would oblige her parents and marry Ralf, but she had no intention of losing Olga. How all this would work was not yet apparent. No matter. Nina was determined to find a way.

She and I now communicated with the five useful words we had picked up from the other's language. The rest was a pantomime patois. When I explained my predicament, she told me that when it comes to sex, women are like camels, able to endure long dry patches. Men, however, are more like cars. Without regular oil changes, their gears grind to a halt. At least I think that's what she said. I'm sure there was a camel in there somewhere. And a car. Anyway, the analogy made perfect sense.

Now, I could have gone all Betty Friedan on her about women's sexual needs, but at the moment I was fixated on locating a good mechanic. Nina had heard rumors about a newly opened gay bar—or at least mixed—in the capital. But the thought of a two-hour train ride and wandering around the capital in search of a well-concealed pub held little appeal—and then only as a last resort. Was there nothing at all closer to home? Not even a dirty tea room?

Almost as an afterthought, she mentioned Luna Park, a notorious nighttime cruising area out near the main highway. Leapin' lizards! A garden of *earthy* delights right here in river city? Normally, I would have dismissed the idea of trolling the bushes for sex. Call me old-fashioned, but bathhouses, toilets, alleys, back rooms, and even phone sex were never my cup of java. I enjoyed frills-free sex as much as the next person back in my single days, but I had to know the person's name, and I insisted on enough face time that I could be reasonably certain he wasn't a psycho.

But someone in the midst of an acute priapic crisis has little time to quibble. *Luna Park here I come.* That evening, I shaved, showered, spritzed myself with Uncle Leonard's citrus-scented cologne, and wended my way to the edge of town, conjuring up images of handsome young sprites frolicking through the glade like a smutty, all-male version of *A Midsummer Night's Dream.*

Unfortunately, this production was all Bottoms (no pun intended) who had already been transformed into donkeys. Luna Park held the decaying remnants of what had been, back in the pre-Soviet era, a charming, modestly scaled amusement area. The carousel just inside the imposing entrance arch was fenced off, the horses lying on their side waiting to be put out of their misery. It was surrounded by other rides that had been left to the mercy of the elements, their paint stripped away and their innards rusted.

The concrete paths separating the rides were littered, and I do mean littered, with sheepish, undoubtedly married middle-aged men who glanced at me and quickly looked away as if horrified by their own urges. Dampness and the fetid odor of desperation permeated the air. By what perversion of the word could any of these men be described as even remotely "gay"?

Hope being a silly creature with spangles on it, I soldiered on. *At least one prince must be lurking among the frogs.* At the center of the park stood an octagonal wooden gazebo on which a gaggle was gathered in a semicircle around an engaged couple. I'm no voyeur. I prefer participatory sports, so I circled back to the entrance just as a boxy vehicle with its lights turned off rolled past. I couldn't be sure, but the bearded Cossack leering at me from behind the wheel as he absent-mindedly fondled himself was a dead ringer for the neighborhood butcher. I fought off a sudden bout of nausea and resolved then and there to buy my meat elsewhere.

Suddenly there were headlights, loud, blaring headlights. An official-looking white and gray police cruiser pulled up, and the men scattered leaving me standing alone like the proverbial cheese. Thinking quick, I improvised a hapless tourist spiel. "Officer, I'm so glad to see you," I said. "I'm a visiting student from America and hopelessly lost. Is this the way to the university library?" The cop snarled and spat out something to the effect of *no speaka da English*, shooing me away like a troublesome child.

On the way home, after I got over my disappointment, I concluded that in a way, the evening had been a success. Sex was now the last thing on my mind, and I had collected enough images of pasty, unattractive men to call upon should the desire return. But my walk on the wild side was not over yet. En route I made a serious wrong turn and ran head-on into an impromptu protest rally (*why oh why oh why oh did I ever leave Ohio?*). Two dozen skinheads carrying torches like the mad peasants in *Frankenstein* and sporting the requisite swastikas and jackboots chanted rage-filled epithets, upending garbage cans and hurling rocks through shop windows. They were flanked by a cordon of policemen who observed in silence. I took refuge in a dark alley and glanced up at the neighbors who were peering nervously from behind curtains in darkened upstairs rooms. Once the marchers passed, the cops got back in their cars, laughing and exchanging pleasantries as if they'd just witnessed an Easter egg roll on someone's front lawn.

The next day I acted out the highlights of my disastrous evening for Nina, who said she was sorry my trip had been a bust, and that she'd never trusted the old Cossack butcher.

Impromptu National Socialism parades, she told me, had become common since the Soviets departed. They were but one of a half dozen political fringe groups that had sprung up in the aftermath of liberation.

As she saw it, freedom can sometimes be overwhelming. Give people too many choices and some will inevitably make the wrong one. Not that she was nostalgic for the Russkies, but at least totalitarianism was disciplined. There were strict parameters about what to think and how to behave. The neo-Nazi protests were merely a manifestation of years of pent-up anger. Everyone still feared the return of Soviet tanks and bombs, but in their absence, the rabble-rousers had turned their wrath on the usual suspects—the intelligentsia, and of course, the Jews.

But according to Olga, there are maybe ten Jews left in town, I mentioned.

Exactly. She nodded. An easy target. We're talking about cowards and lunatics, she sneered, not forward-thinking patriots.

Gotta love that Nina. Always cuts right to the chase.

Sad to say, the dampening effect on my sex drive after the Luna Park debacle proved to be temporary. The weather wasn't exactly balmy, but the days were getting warmer and longer, and healthy exposure to sunlight lifted my spirits and replenished my juices. The streets no longer seemed as ominous and constricting. On many days I was able to coax a smile out of even dour shopkeepers who, I guess, no longer regarded me as suspect.

I wasn't the only one craving affection. Finals be damned, Olga managed to wedge in the occasional quickie with Nina in the storage room behind the café before scurrying back to her textbooks. When Nina told her about my sojourn in Luna Park, she grimaced.

"Luna Park is for…" Olga made an "L" with her thumb and forefinger. Nina was understandably perplexed. "Just do it. Matthew he know what it means," she said. Then, bless her little heart, Olga suggested I try the Turkish baths just off the city's main drag. Nina scoffed. The baths are just a bunch of saggy old coots in towels taking a steam and swimming naked in the hot mineral pools, she argued. Her father was a regular and had never once mentioned carryings-on.

Nonetheless, on the slim chance that Olga was on to something, I headed downtown to the Moorish-style building with its immaculate interior of shiny green, white, and black tile. A cupola dotted with bright Cyrillic script rose over a teal-bottomed central swimming pool. At midday the bathhouse was teeming with furry old men *shvitzing* and *kibitzing*, shuffling along in their scuffies wrapped in giant white towels like ancient Roman senators. Oh well, I thought, my heart sinking. Guess I'll just have to settle for a pore-cleansing steam and maybe a happy-ending-less massage.

After a quick skinny dip, I vanished into the dense fog of the all-white tiled steam room. Feeling around for a place to sit, I had no sooner undraped and heaved a contented sigh than an unseen hand groped me. Startled, I grabbed my towel and blindly stumbled out. Don't ask me why when an obliging stranger offered to take my problem in hand, I absconded, glancing worriedly over my shoulder like I was being pursued by Jack the Ripper through the back alleys of London.

Then I heard a soft voice call out to me. "Hello, American. Why you run away?"

Leaning against the far wall was a tall man with a winsome grin, linebacker shoulders, soulful basset hound eyes, and a wiggly little mustache.

"How do you know I'm American?"

"My friend at entrance he say to me, 'Find the young American.'" He smiled, raising his eyebrows suggestively. "My name Walter. You come. We take steam."

And I did. Not necessarily in that order.

Chapter Seven
Rich Man, Poor Man

After one final marathon session with Lawyer Bombyk, the transfer of Uncle Leonard's assets was completed. He made one last pitch to let him manage the estate. I politely declined, and he gave me one of those have-it-your-way shoulder shrugs and curtly dismissed me with a wave of the hand.

My first stop was Uncle Leonard's bank downtown, a faceless establishment that looked less like a financial institution than a customs house. The top floors of the building had once been home to the local branch of the KGB, according to Nina.

If these walls could talk... On second thought, I prefer not to know.

There were no tellers' cages in this bank, merely a long mahogany counter behind which stood a man dressed like an undertaker with his hair neatly parted down the middle. The customers sat on a backless bench and were waited on in shifts. First, your name was called, and after a brief interchange, you were directed back to your seat as the banker/mortician fastidiously scribbled something on a scrap of paper and presented it to the young woman at the desk behind him. Then the next person was summoned. And so on.

When my turn arrived, he leaned on one elbow and crumpled his brow, studying the transfer papers as if he was decoding the Dead Sea Scrolls. He held up my passport and compared the admittedly awful photo—my face was very puffy that day—to the young man in front of him. He directed me back to the bench and disappeared, returning a few minutes later with an older gentleman who sported an Austrian psychiatrist's goatee. They spent the next fifteen minutes in rapid-paced, hush-toned conversation occasionally tossing me a wary glance as if they expected me to crack at any moment and confess to a heinous crime, all for what amounted to a one-hundred-dollar withdrawal.

My right foot kicked nervously against the side of the bench the way it does when my seven-year-olds are acting up after a sugar-rush lunch. The confab finally ended with nods and a sweeping John Hancock flourish. The funereal teller placed the signed paper under a cashier's nose. Without looking up, she flipped open a lockbox and counted out several large bills, the value of paper money here being inversely proportional to its size.

"Robins," he intoned, glaring at me as he begrudgingly slipped the cash into my passport and inched it across the counter, almost daring me to take possession.

On the way home, I stopped at the town's one and only hardware store and purchased a heavy-duty flashlight. The afternoon's entertainment would include a visit to the inner depths of the commercial space adjacent to 222, which to my understanding housed a former carpentry shop. As I attacked the rusted padlock in the downstairs hallway, I sensed the old lady squinting at me through a crack in the double doors. After several failed attempts, one of the silver keys slipped into the aperture and hesitantly clicked. I pressed my shoulder against the bloated wooden door, and it opened with a sharp thwack, pulling away part of the frame.

The moment I set foot inside, the old witch threw open the doors and began hurling curses at me, probably ancient gypsy hexes. With a victorious smile, I turned, waved, and slammed the door on her, leaving me in complete darkness. *Nice going, Matt.*

Clicking on the flashlight, I located a light switch, which I assumed would be juiceless after all these years. Not so. Icy-blue fluorescent tubes crackled to life, revealing a dust-covered, damp room whose whitewashed walls had faded to a discomfiting shade of gray and sported patches of hairy mold. Water had seeped under the floor at some point, buckling the linoleum, which crunched and split under my feet.

As I surveyed the room, I realized that the carpentry shop had at some point been replaced by an eating and/or drinking establishment. Strewn about the room were marble-topped wrought-iron based tables, wooden chairs with cane seats and a serving counter, also marble, running the length of the far wall. From the looks of it, the place had closed down in a hurry. The tables were stacked with dirty dishes and glassware, the chairs turned every which way.

The walls were hung with photos and illustrations obscured beneath a layer of dust. I found a clean dishrag behind the counter and wiped one of them, which looked like a portrait of Dwight Eisenhower, though it could just as well have been some local bald-headed commissar. The second photo, however, was unmistakably Ike, his chest weighed down with medals. Next to it hung a 1955 calendar of the president and First Lady Mamie.

Curiouser and curiouser.

I turned with a start when I heard the door squeak open

behind me, expecting to see Broomhilda. A tall, lumpy man waddled in, his face plastered with a leery smile.

"Good day to you," he said with a nervous laugh, doffing his cap and extending his hand. "I am Viktor, son of Martina and Peter," he added, pointing to the apartment behind him.

For a moment I was confused since Lawyer Bombyk hadn't told me the tenant's actual names and I foolishly never bothered to ask. *Martina and Peter. Got it.*

Viktor had narrow, almond-shaped eyes like his mother, which made them hard to read, but also a square jaw of decency.

"Matthew Robins," I said, shaking his hand, "Leonard's nephew, grand-nephew, actually."

"Yes, I know this from Bombyk," Viktor said as he gazed up at the hammered tin ceiling. "I have not been inside here since I was young boy."

"So I guess this place was a café?"

"Something like. Club for men to talk, maybe to play cards. On Sunday the wives they come too. My father he work here and, sometimes if it is very busy, I help to wash dishes, which I break more than I clean." He punctuated his account with a forced titter.

"It seems to have been abandoned all of a sudden."

"This is true, yes."

"What happened?"

He looked down at his cap and twirled it around in his hand. "The police. They say people come here to discuss politics. But not true. They talk yes, but of life problems and in those days, many problems. First the war and the Germans and the Russians who, when war is finished, remain. We are not free country. No one happy. Police think any time people together, is to make trouble. They close and open and close again. Then no open no more."

"So, how long was the café in operation?"

"One, almost two years. Uncle he go to complain—complain is right?—to magistrate but…" He sighed and looked down at the floor. "Perhaps not good idea to put picture of American president on wall."

"But he was also a general and a hero. He helped end the war."

"Soviets maybe not like to be reminded of this. They think they win war."

"I see. So, are you in some way related to my uncle?"

"Oh no," he said taking a step back. "I call him uncle for respect. He old friend with my father. They like brothers. Uncle very good to my family. He teach me to speak English…"

And this, ladies and gents, was my *aha* moment. Could Isaac and Tonio actually be Uncle Leonard and Peter? Now I really couldn't wait for Olga to get back to the notebooks.

"Your English is very good," I told Viktor.

"Most kind of you to say," he responded, pleased and slightly embarrassed. "Uncle good teacher. He professor of English at university."

"Something else I didn't know."

Other questions suddenly popped into my head, but we were interrupted by Martina, who growled at her son from the doorway but averted her eyes as if she feared the room might be filled with ghosts. And if what I suspected was true, it was.

"Matthew, is mean Matejus, yes? A pleasure to meet you," Victor said as he slowly backed out of the room. "Please to have patience. My mother have difficult life and papa is not well." He tapped his temple suggesting that the old man's woes might extend beyond the physical. "I hope to see you again and thank you for honoring uncle's wishes for my family."

"I wish I'd known him."

"He good man. In many ways."

Viktor retreated into his parents' apartment and a few minutes later, a sharp car horn honked outside. Through the wooden slats over the café window, I noticed a robust young man in military-style olive drabs and beret jump out of a jeep-like vehicle and scoop up Martina. She showered him with kisses, the first time I'd ever seen her express any emotion other than rage. Viktor emerged from the house pushing Peter in the wheelchair. After boosting Martina into the backseat, the young man lifted Peter and deposited him next to her while Viktor folded up the wheelchair and secured it to the back of the vehicle. As they drove away, I mulled over Viktor's last remark. Uncle Leonard was a good man "in many ways," he said. In what ways was he not a good man? Perhaps in his affection for Peter?

Calm down, Matt. You're getting way ahead of yourself.

❖

Despite my promise to Caroline that I would take "tons of pictures" with her old Leica, it was still sitting in my suitcase. But today I was traveling to the capital, so I took the camera out and loaded it.

My first official photo was of Olga and Nina huddled together on the train, looking as if they were on their way to the gallows. I asked them to smile and say cheese, but to little avail. "Try to think of a cheese you like, preferably not limburger," I suggested. No use.

On the way, I told them about Viktor, the short-lived café and my theory about Peter's "friendship" with Uncle Leonard, aka Tonio and Isaac.

"Is possible," Olga conceded. "If true, it is a sad story."

Nina, as expected, was skeptical. She preferred to view

the notebooks as wish fulfillment, the suggestion being that young boys didn't do things like that back in the day.

"You're right. You and Olga discovered gay sex," I said with a snort. But she held her ground.

Our day in the big city was planned in part to celebrate Olga passing her finals—with distinction no less. We also planned to shop for Nina's trousseau, do some sightseeing, and hunt down the alleged gay bar.

The capital suggested Old World splendor, though it, too, had fallen victim to decades of neglect: cracked red tile roofs and crumbling Art Nouveau–style buildings of glass and stone; snaking narrow lanes blocked with debris that fed into once opulent open squares. Here and there were tentative signs of new life—the occasional al fresco café or scaffolding on what had once undoubtedly been pomp-and-circumstance government buildings. Some were in the process of being restored, others were being razed to make way for modern glass-and-steel structures. At least that's what the photo banners on their façades suggested. One unmistakable sign of progress was the traffic jam, with little Russian-made bug cars, stuffed with hunched-over men and women.

The lumbering bunker we were standing in front of was, according to Nina, a former Soviet department store that had been taken over by a popular German clothing chain and was said to carry all the latest fashions. Her assessment turned out to be uncharacteristically generous. The interior of the three-story structure was stark and underlit and made Filene's Basement look like the palace at Versailles. The salesladies greeted us with all the charm of prison matrons, though not as elegantly coiffed.

Since neither Nina nor Olga showed the least enthusiasm about the trousseau, I volunteered. First stop, ladies' lingerie, a major disappointment consisting mostly of generously cut white and pink "bloomers" that in a pinch could be used as makeshift sail on a skiff. The bras were industrial design with clumsy fishhook fasteners.

The dress department's spring collection consisted of a dozen variations on the same unflattering silhouette in decidedly autumnal browns, oxbloods, and inky, dark blues. Any woman who stepped out on the town in one of these high-necked, long-sleeved ensembles needn't worry her pretty head about birth control.

As for the ladies' footwear, the boxes holding the shoes had more style. I believe the appropriate word here is "clodhoppers."

Except for some embossed Irish linen handkerchiefs, we left the store empty-handed. On our way toward the city's main square, however, we lucked into a cluster of specialty shops (to call them boutiques would be an overstatement) and managed to scrape together an ensemble that flattered Nina's svelte physique with enough contemporary-ish flair that she wouldn't look like she was stepping out in her mother's hand-me-downs. Despite their indifference, Olga and Nina thanked me for my efforts, though truthfully, when it comes to fashion I confess to being a rank amateur. I have a few stylish pieces in my wardrobe but only because Nathaniel and sometimes Caroline picked them out for me. My personal tastes don't run much past J.Crew and Ralph Lauren, decidedly preppy and a bit constipated.

One of the memorable photos I took that day was of Nina at the bridal shop emerging from the dressing room in an explosion of lace. Fortunately since I was behind the camera, Nina couldn't see the look of horror on my face when she cooed that her mother had worn almost the exact same gown at her wedding. "Then why not pull Mom's dress out of mothballs instead of plunking down beaucoup bucks for something you're only going to wear once anyway?" I argued.

"Because is bad luck. Bad luck," Olga explained. "Her mother have terrible marriage," she said, which again reminded her of Nina's pending nuptials, and she began sobbing uncontrollably. Nina soon joined her. The icy saleslady, mistaking their outpouring for tears of joy, only made things worse when she crowed, "She will be even more beautiful the day she walks down the aisle."

"Is worse than to die," Olga said to me, repeating the phrase in her native tongue to the saleslady who again misunderstood.

"If a woman is smart she can make husband happy and herself," she counseled, patting Nina's shoulder. When Olga translated, I cracked up. Soon we were all laughing, including the poor saleslady, who would have been appalled if she suspected how close she'd come to the truth.

Another favorite snapshot was of Nina and Olga fumbling with chopsticks. By accident we happened on a Chinese restaurant, and after months of nothing but meat pies and heavy stews, the mere thought of roast pork fried rice was aphrodisiacal. My treat, I announced.

As always, Olga was game, while Nina was convinced we were about to dine on sauced-over rodents and house pets. It didn't help that as we entered a scraggly kitty limped by and disappeared into the alley behind the restaurant.

I'm the first to admit that it wasn't the best Chinese food I've ever had, barely passable Cantonese, the kind I abandoned after discovering the far superior Mandarin, Szechuan, and Hunan. To my surprise, Nina quickly got the hang of using chopsticks, though she scoffed at using wooden poles to push food into your mouth when there were perfectly good metal utensils available. Olga, who is not usually a picky eater, turned up her nose at almost every dish except for wontons, pot stickers, and the egg rolls, which made perfect sense since her daily diet leaned heavily toward pastry-encrusted meats.

The rest of the afternoon was devoted to hunting down the alleged lavender tavern. After going around in circles several times, we finally stumbled on the place, which was located in the industrial section of town, sequestered down a dark side street not much wider than an alley. The bar was below street level behind an unmarked door guarded by a bouncer so scrawny that any of the three of us could have taken him. The constricted, overheated space had a tiny dance floor at the back complete with the obligatory mirrored ball. But at least the music, '70s Euro-tech, was welcoming.

The patrons of this fair establishment were overwhelmingly male, including a few frumpily dressed transvestites who obviously frequented the German-based fashion emporium. They all clustered in tight-knit cliques and, as in most gay bars, pretended to be having a great time with their friends when what they truly desired was to be swept off their feet by a charismatic stranger. Being the new kids in town, we were greeted with the glances of disdain. We practically had to mug the bartender before he deigned to serve us.

To memorialize our outing, I whipped out the Leica and asked Olga and Nina to strike a pose. When the flash went off, several men ducked or turned away in panic like Bela Lugosi at the first glimmer of dawn. The bartender shook his fist at us but eventually backed off after Olga screamed him down. "We're not interested in photographing your ugly face or anybody else's, so leave us the fuck alone." Or words to that effect.

The drinks were expensive and heavily watered down, and it took quite a few before my companions were loosened up enough to be lured onto the dance floor. As we boogied, my roving eye fell on a pleasant-looking chap who for some strange reason was wearing a cap with ear flaps. When I smiled at him, he became apoplectic and made a beeline for the exit. I checked the mirror to see if I had chicken chow mein stuck in my teeth.

Though it was hands down the most downtrodden gay bar I'd ever visited, Olga and Nina spoke of little else on the way home. The opportunity to slow dance together without comment or censure was like finding the other side of paradise. Even I was forced to admit that it represented a giant step forward from the squelched panic of Luna Park or the secrecy of the Turkish baths, except for dear sweet Walter, with whom I now regularly steamed. And I had the clean pores to prove it.

Having exhausted all my reasons to remain in Eastern Europe, I began contemplating my return trip, though I promised to stay until Nina's wedding, which I wouldn't have missed for the world. Olga and I spoke to a real estate agent about renting out my uncle's apartment, the proceeds of which would go toward utilities and maintenance. Then after Peter passed or moved away, I'd put the property up for sale and figure out what to do with the money.

A few nights later, a major neo-Nazi rally happened right outside Luna Park. The usual battery of policemen casually stood by as the skinheads marched through town spewing hatred and animosity. This time, however, the neighbors came out of their houses to confront them. Push came to shove, shove came to punches. Windows were smashed and a couple of homemade Molotovs were tossed, setting a car on fire. The cops were finally forced to intervene, but instead of going after the protesters, they decided to arrest the hapless cruisers. In the aftermath of the incident, the park was permanently shuttered after sundown.

"Poor schnooks," I lamented. "Now where are they going to go to be miserable?"

Then Olga had an epiphany. "Wait, I know what we do," she said, looking up from the third notebook, which she had just started translating. She breathlessly outlined a plan that any sane person would have immediately rejected—to renovate the café as a haven for gays, where they could gather in a safe, open environment. She would run the establishment and Nina would serve as hostess.

Playing devil's advocate, I said, "And Ralf would not be at all suspicious that his blushing bride has decided to quit her steady job to cater to queers?"

"Ralf, he understands nothing," Olga scoffed. "He sees only what it is convenient for him." I couldn't argue with her. If Olga was constantly mooning over my fiancée, I'd sure as heck notice. But as we all know, denial can be a powerful mechanism.

I mulled over Olga's proposal. But instead of dismissing it, in a moment of sheer lunacy, I chimed, "Sure, why not? Let's go for it."

Your honor, I plead temporary insanity aggravated by grief and a steady diet of indigestible meat pies.

Starting a new business provided me with the perfect excuse to place my departure on indefinite hold. Reopening the café was clearly one of the reasons I had been summoned to Eastern Europe, I told myself. It had to have been foreordained. Otherwise, why would I have run into that guy Sam from Ohio who bragged about making a real estate killing in Czechoslovakia?

Besides, I owed it to Uncle Leonard. In my fevered imagination, he had intuited a common bond with the American great-nephew he didn't even know existed, and willed him all his earthly possessions. That decision in turn had led to the discovery of the notebooks detailing a possible secret affair. Whether the notebooks were true or merely an unrealized dream, restoring the café would be his vindication from the beyond.

I even incorporated Nathaniel and my mother into this convenient rationalization. Since she and Nathaniel had probably run into each other up in the afterlife, it made sense they would eventually connect with Uncle Leonard. And who did the three of them have in common? I could practically feel my ears burning.

The contents of the third notebook only reaffirmed my belief that I was on the right path.

NOTEBOOK THREE (1945)

When Tonio awakens, for a moment he believes that he has reached paradise. He is lying in a room bathed in a celestial glow. He attempts to raise his right hand to shield his eyes, but it is curiously weighted and he can barely lift it from his side. Eventually, the sun retreats behind a cloud and the light softens. His eyes have time to adjust, and he discovers that he is in a long white-walled room with beds on either side. The other men in the room are all fast asleep even though it is clearly the middle of the day.

Perhaps he is not in paradise at all but merely in limbo, a middle state for the unbaptized and those whose souls still need to be cleansed of the residue of sin. If so, it is a lovely place to begin eternity. Commanding all his strength, he raises his head a few inches from the pillow and glances through the window on his right.

Outside are tall bushes bearing waxy

red berries swaying easily in the breeze. His lungs ingest the cool fresh air, which is almost immediately superseded by the pungent odor of antiseptics. Then his energy flags, and he has to lay his head back down. A sudden excruciating pain surges through his left leg. He balls his fists and prays that it will stop. Must there be suffering in the afterlife too? Perhaps it is something he must endure before he is fully absolved of his sins. Then he will be ready to begin eternity.

Presently, there are footsteps. A woman in a white bonnet moves quietly from bed to bed monitoring the sleeping young men. Madam, he whispers as she approaches, and the woman starts.

You gave me a fright, she gently admonishes him. I have been waiting for you, she adds, as if he'd just returned from his morning constitutional.

Am I dead? he inquires. The moment he speaks it, he's struck by how foolish the question sounds when uttered aloud.

You are very much alive, more alive than you've been for several months, she gently assures him.

Tonio learns that he was gravely wounded in a battle against the Germans, and that the doctors labored for several hours to retrieve him from the brink of death. His left leg was badly damaged, and chunks of shrapnel are still embedded in his skull, only an inch from the brain. After a time in hospital, when he still had not regained consciousness, he was moved here, along with dozens of men in similar conditions, some of whom are also expected to revive eventually. The others, she notes soberly, are simply in transit.

Tonio wishes he could recall when he was injured and the events that preceded it. Shortly after he joined the army, it fell under German command. He was involved in several skirmishes, some against his own countrymen, which he found intolerable. Without his father's knowledge, he deserted and joined the resistance, and they hid in the forest up north. He could still smell the dampness and the softness of lichen and fungi underfoot as he and the other members of the brigade went about their daily maneuvers, which mostly consisted of foraging for food. He has no idea how long he served with the renegade militia, nor can he remember whether he was wounded in an all-out attack or a minor ambush.

What is this place? he asks the woman. A large country villa, she tells him, the estate of a noble family, which has been appropriated because the hospitals are overcrowded with the freshly wounded. You are one of but a handful to have emerged from the ether, each of you a small miracle.

Let us give thanks, she says, and Tonio mumbles along as she recites a Hail Mary over him. Following her Amen, she tells him she is going to fetch the doctor, who will come by to examine him. He will be so pleased that you are awake and, hopefully, will let me know when you're well enough to eat solid food. We must fatten you up before sending you back to your wife, she laughs, noting the gold band on his fourth finger.

As the soft crunch of her shoes across the wooden floor fades, Tonio closes his eyes and wonders if Isaac has already given him up for dead and whether his wife, Alla, has given birth to their child.

The marriage was hastily arranged in the early days of the war. Alla's father was a magistrate who had befriended Edvard's father. Edvard had first proposed the match, which he viewed as a potentially significant step in his continued political ascent. Alla was older than Tonio, a sober, God-fearing young woman, his father assured him. They were only introduced to one another a week before their wedding day, mainly so their families might come to a financial agreement, which included a substantial dowry. The ceremony was a rushed affair since Tonio had been granted leave only for the afternoon and was expected back in his regiment by nightfall. They didn't even have time to consummate the union. At the small supper following the ceremony, Tonio regarded Alla with what she likely interpreted as quiet desire. But, in fact, he was trying to imagine what Isaac would make of his bride. His friend was a quick study and a keen judge of character. He always knew how to ask exactly the right questions to plumb a person's true nature.

Even if Isaac had not been forced to flee and war had been averted, eventually their families would have found them wives. Tonio believed that the current tide of virulent anti-Semitism would gradually subside, part of a continuous historical ebb and flow. In the days before they were separated, he assured Isaac that when things returned to normal, a friendship between their families would no longer be regarded as beyond the pale, either politically or socially. Regardless, the bond between them would remain constant and indissoluble for the rest of their lives. On that much at least, they concurred.

Now, faced with the prospect that Isaac might never return despite his solemn vow to do so, Tonio was forced to re-examine his life. During his first leave several weeks after the marriage, he made every effort to establish a rapport with his wife. Conjugally, she was largely what he had expected, inexperienced yet compliant. She also proved to be fecund, becoming pregnant during that first and only visit. He received the news at the front via a tersely scrawled note in which Alla expressed neither pleasure nor discontent. But then she was not a very expressive woman, having been educated at a convent school that stressed silence as the ultimate female virtue.

Though he is not yet aware of it, during his extended convalescence, Tonio's world has again changed and not to his advantage. The previous political order has been upended. His father and father-in-law were branded German collaborators by the newly installed pro-Soviet government. Tonio's mother and sister now reside in the country living off an aunt's charity. Alla and the infant he has not yet seen, a boy named Dag, have moved in with her maternal grandparents and are skirting starvation.

After the armistice is declared, and Tonio has fully recovered, he is officially discharged. He is unable to complete his studies at the university since he must now scramble to support his wife and child. The family name is in eclipse and most of his friends who survived the war have turned their backs on him. The only one who extends himself, Pyotr, a fellow classmate, offers him a lowly clerk position in the family haberdashery and constantly reminds him of his kindness. Tonio is not a proud man, but he feels a certain shame in barely being able to provide for his family. He would never want Isaac to see him reduced to such circumstances.

Tonio writes several letters to Isaac but never posts them. If Isaac did indeed reach America, he is unlikely to return now that his family has been eliminated and their war-savaged homeland has fallen into Russian hands. To communicate with his beloved knowing he will never see him again would be unbearable. Worse is the fear that Isaac might pity him. So he decides to redirect his energies and strive to become a suitable husband and, more importantly, a good father to Dag.

One Saturday afternoon, after standing in a food queue for three hours with Dag balanced on his shoulders, he sees someone who resembles Isaac walk past the shop window and considers pursuing him. It is not the first such sighting, though none of the previous phantoms proved to be his absent friend. Fool, he thinks, you must stop conjuring him up in every passerby. You must force yourself to forget and move forward.

Chapter Eight
Any Place I Hang My Hat

I suppose that if I hadn't stumbled on the notebooks, I would have found another excuse to open the café. I wasn't simply stalling for time. After the initial shock of adjusting to an alien environment rife with abysmal weather, hostile natives, and terrible food, I had acclimated. The absence of responsibilities and concrete reminders of my life with Nathaniel made Long Island seem like a distant shore. It helped that the days had turned warmer, that I'd made friends and adapted to the diet— though I would have killed for a green salad some days. For better, and for worse, I was beginning to feel peculiarly at home in this foreign land.

The cliffhanger ending of the third notebook left me famished for the next installment. But this time I smacked up against an emotional roadblock. As Nina's nuptials neared, Olga sank deeper and deeper into a rage-filled depression. Though she claimed to be suicidal, I saw little evidence of that, unless she was planning to eat herself to death. Olga is not one to suffer in silence and if she was unhappy, the rest of us shouldn't even consider cracking a smile. Woe to the passerby who unintentionally bumped into her or the tradesman who didn't move fast enough with her order. She reamed them like the master drill sergeant in *Full Metal Jacket*. We're talking scary.

Meanwhile, Nina blithely prepared for her wedding day as if her husband-to-be was but a mere hiccup in the pursuit of her true heart's desire. "Once I am married," she consoled Olga, "no one will pay me any mind because I belong to my husband. And since I will become Ralf's servant, he will have no need to speak to me, except to express his wishes." Her sobering assessment of the matrimonial state finally penetrated Olga's thick skull, though outwardly she continued to grouse and throw tantrums. Nina gently coaxed her into being my plus-one at the wedding, for which she'd commandeered me as official photographer. "You have camera. You have film. You take pictures," she insisted.

The ceremony marked Olga's first adult public appearance in a dress. She even had her hair coifed and her nails painted. The end effect was dispiriting, to say the least. I've seen daintier Sumo wrestlers. It's not that she looked like a transvestite; no, nothing as glamorous or illusory as that. Black jeans, boots, and a motorcycle jacket gave her a tough-gal, sexy swagger, but more feminine garb neutered her.

"You look lovely," I said when I picked her up in front of the beauty salon. "You lie like a rug." She frowned, tugging at her nylons and hobbling along in her pinching heels. That's what I get for teaching her idioms.

Nina's wedding was no brown-bag affair. Ralf came from a family of means. His uncle, the local bishop, officiated at the Catholic high mass at a massive Baroque cathedral, providing the perfect photo op—a roaring soprano, incense, and tons of audience participation. From the portentous downbeat of the giant pipe organ reverberating through the massive nave as sweet cherubs sprinkled flowers up the aisle, to the final glorious crescendo as the happy couple marched triumphantly out of the basilica, I was enthralled.

No wonder Catholicism has enjoyed an unprecedented

two-thousand-year run. They've got all the best liturgical music and art, not to mention the niftiest interior design, enormous stained glass windows and tons and tons of gilt. The statuary alone was worth the price of admission, my favorites being the decapitated martyr holding his head on a platter and, of course, the steamy, mostly naked Sebastian, shot through with arrows, his eyes rolling around in S&M ecstasy. The fathers of the church knew exactly what they were doing. The eroticism is much too overt to be accidental. I mean, who needs Barry White when you've got Mozart's *Requiem* and statues of well-defined saints in various states of undress?

Since I had been conscripted into committing the day to posterity, I carefully deposited Olga in a rear pew out of harm's way, far enough from the altar that I'd have fair warning if she suddenly decided to do something rash like bolt up the aisle and try to abscond with Nina. The university had recently screened *The Graduate* and Olga was particularly susceptible to suggestion.

Despite her sartorial and psychological discomfort, Olga was fairly well behaved until after the "I dos" were exchanged. Then, as if it had just dawned on her, she groused to me that Ralf now had permission to venture where no man had ever gone before with her precious Nina.

"Relax," I whispered. "Nina could sleep with the entire Fifth Fleet and she'd still be true to you. Remember, it's not about what happens between her legs that counts. It's what's going on between her ears."

I meant it too. Heck, if Nathaniel had been forced to marry a woman, the last thing on my mind would have been the physical act. The real intimacy is what happens before and after. That he might share those moments with anyone else, male or female, is what would have driven me round the bend.

Despite her *sangfroid* exterior, Nina didn't appear to be enjoying her wedding day any more than Olga. Suffocated in lace, the rigid, waxen figure who walked up the aisle on her father's arm was but a pale replica of the sly, formidable Nina I'd come to know and love. Truly. If I was forced to cohabit with a woman, Nina would be my first choice. The girl's got serious chops. Don't get me wrong, I'm very fond of Olga. But I'm sorry, she's too high-maintenance.

Nina uttered her vows in a dull, barely audible voice, never once making eye contact with Ralf. Even when he lifted the veil for the obligatory first kiss, she stared over his shoulder the entire time. She'd kissed me with more enthusiasm.

As the newlyweds departed, Nina conspicuously avoided eye contact with Olga. I guess she was afraid she might lose her cool. But on the way out, Ralf, the original Mr. Oblivious, glared directly at Olga, and I saw his upper lip curl.

At the reception, Olga merely picked at her food as I plied her with flutes of champagne and vodka, which made her lethargic and wistful, allowing me the freedom to move around the hall taking pictures of the assembled guests. What a bunch of stiffs. The custom of smiling for the camera had obviously never reached these shores, nor had the concept of the "candid" pose. If this is how these folks appear in a celebratory mode, hope I never have to attend one of their funerals.

Olga's pouting only served as a reminder that she was still a fragile girl of nineteen and, like her peers, completely flummoxed by the incendiary nature of romance.

"I want to cry but I am too angry," Olga blurted. "I must go to Nina to save her."

"Sit there and do not move a muscle," I commanded. "Stalking Nina and Ralf is not the answer. Try a little empathy.

Think of what poor Nina has to endure on the honeymoon. On second thought, don't think about it. Have some more vodka."

After I'd gotten her good and desensitized, I dragged Olga's carcass home and put her to bed with the help of her older brother, Alexei.

Alexei was my new best friend and de facto contractor. He'd been gifted with the same stocky physique as Olga, though it was better distributed on his frame. Like his sister, Alexei possessed a certain gruff charm and was also a bit of a know-it-all. He'd worked briefly in construction and claimed to have a bead on all the best tradesmen in town. He talked their talk, he assured me, and guaranteed that my project would get top priority if I was willing to pony up incentives. Alexei's negotiating skills entailed a great deal of palm greasing, not merely for the laborers and craftsmen but also the legion of municipal inspectors and licensors. I doubt that the construction of a Las Vegas casino necessitates as many inspections and permits.

"This is how business is done here, my friend," Alexei argued every time I balked at another under-the-table sop. Olga, who served as interpreter, nodded in agreement, strangely docile in her brother's presence. The main reason I caved was because I regarded the local currency as Monopoly money. Also I'm not the world's most astute financial planner, as Nathaniel would have been the first to acknowledge.

I was now making almost daily withdrawals from the bank downtown and was soon on a first-name basis with the undertaker/teller Dmitri. We came to an understanding around the time I showed up with home-baked oatmeal cookies for him and the other employees. The first time I offered him a cookie, Dmitri's reaction was almost priceless. He studied it and sniffed at it suspiciously, and I flashed him a huge smile and, confident that he didn't understand a word a word of English said, "Go ahead, try it. It's loaded with cyanide. You won't feel a thing." After the first tentative bite, he gobbled it down, and when I handed him the entire tin, his eyes sparkled like it was a bowl of pure-cut Colombian.

To keep myself busy while I was supervising the tradesmen, I assumed the responsibility of painting the café.

"All by yourself?" said Caroline during one of our weekly chats. "Funny, because I recall asking you to help me redo my bathroom and you got all limp-wristed on me."

"That's because I didn't want you breathing over my shoulder micromanaging every brush stroke."

"Busted," she conceded.

When I shared my concept for the café, Caroline was unimpressed. "If I was grading you on originality in coping with your loss, I'd say B+ or A-. That is, if I was in a giving mood," she said, using that tone she reserved for her more obstreperous pupils. "But I'm not. So I'm giving you a C. Opening a gay café in Eastern Europe is noble but misguided. Your heart's in the right place. It's your head that's not screwed on tight."

"Thank you for being a friend," I said.

"Don't be that way. It's not as if I gave you a failing grade," she argued. "Plenty of C students go on to illustrious careers, even the presidency. Look at Jimmy Carter. So how long before you work this out of your system and come home?"

"I take the Fifth."

"That's what you said the last time I asked and the time before that," she said, a little frostiness in her voice. "And until you have a different answer to that question, I'm going to screen my calls."

"Don't take it personally," I said. "It's not as if I don't miss you."

"Why would I take it personally that my best friend is avoiding his life?" Then she took a deep breath and melted. "I guess you'll come home when you come home."

"And that's why I love you," I chirped.

"So tell me some more about your new life as Pete the Painter. How much of it actually gets on the walls?"

"Very funny," I snapped. "I'll have you know I'm making great strides. The neighbors seem to be impressed. People come from miles around just to applaud my technique. Well, actually just one person. And I'm pretty sure he's a government spy."

Dead silence on the other end of the line. Caroline was probably picturing me at a show trial, head bowed in front of a tribunal, wearing a large sign around my paint-spattered neck on which the words "Capitalist idiot" were scrawled.

"When you say government spy, can you be more specific?"

"'Fraid not. Thus far I haven't actually seen him, only his silhouette lurking in the shadows across the way."

"Then how do you know he's a spy? He could just be a creep."

"It's just a hunch. Do you think a creep would have the patience to just stand around all day and watch me paint? I know there's not much in the way of entertainment around here, but that's a bit of stretch."

"Should I be worried?" she asked in a sheepish tone.

"Why? I've got nothing to hide."

"Oh yeah? When you applied for a license, how did you describe the café?"

"Just your run-of-the-mill coffee house. Strictly speaking that's not a lie. Everyone's welcome. It's not as if I'm taking a survey of sexual orientation at the door. Now I've got to say good-bye. It's time to give a second coat to the kitchen."

"Okay, but you've got to promise to call me more often. Once a week is not enough."

"That could run into serious shekels."

"Call collect. I'm serious. I don't want my best friend to become a *desaparecido*."

"Wrong continent, but I appreciate the sentiment. *Do svidaniya*, baby."

"So not funny," Caroline fumed, and there was a loud click.

For someone who fancies himself a keen observer of his environment, until Nina brought it to my attention, I had been blithely unaware that my daily routine was being scrutinized. "Someone watching," she pantomimed.

My first thought was someone from the painter's union.

"Maybe is police," Nina added in that subtle way she has of detonating explosives.

I should explain that, initially, Nina had been dead set against the concept for the café. As with her clandestine partnership with Olga, Nina was a firm believer in flying under the radar. To this day, I doubt she'd identify as lesbian or even bisexual. She is merely in love with a woman named Olga and not with the man who'd been chosen to be her husband. Since returning from her honeymoon, she'd warmed up to the idea but not because she was ready to get her freak on. The prospect of spending more time with Olga and less with Ralf, was simply too tantalizing to resist.

She'd bravely suffered through her marital duties during the honeymoon, she told me with a wide yawn. "Ralf, he is Ralf," she said, which told me everything and nothing at the same time. When I later pressed Olga, she informed me that Nina's new husband had been mercifully brief. He'd clearly never heard of foreplay, or the idea of delaying gratification by thinking of soccer stats. Nina, who had technically been a virgin, closed her eyes and thought of England or the regional equivalent, but never of Olga, lest she get excited, which would send the wrong message to her bridegroom.

By now, Nina and I had made considerable progress and were engaging in genuine if somewhat ersatz conversations. We'd each learned the rudiments of the other's language, she more so than stubbornly monolingual me. Hand motions and facial gestures filled in the gaps, an acknowledgment of our evolved simian roots.

When Nina first told me I was being watched, I was about to turn my head when she flashed the universal stop sign—the palm of her hand—and said, "Matejus. Be cool."

Pretending that I needed a good stretch, I got down from the ladder, ambled outside, and loitered at the curb, shaking my hands and legs like I was limbering up for yoga class. An angular figured swathed in shadow and smoking a cigarette eyed me from across the way, a no-goodnik right out of Graham Greene or Eric Ambler minus the trench coat and fedora. When I move toward him for a closer look, he flicked his cigarette, took a step back, and was swallowed up by the darkness.

Next day he was back and every morning after that, though whenever I approached, he immediately turned tail. After a few rounds of cat-and-mouse, I resolved to ignore him. If his idea of fun was watching me prime walls, who was I to drip paint on his parade? Even if he was working for the police, what was he going to do, denounce me for splattering?

One lazy morning, I decided to break early for lunch. At the upstairs window in my apartment as I noshed on a ham and cheese sandwich and washed it down with a bottle of cool ale, my personal spy emerged from his lair to examine my handiwork close-up. I grabbed Uncle Leonard's opera glasses from a shelf in the closet and crouched down on my haunches so he wouldn't see me.

Hubba, hubba! Oh baby, you can spy on me anytime you want.

I'm guessing he was maybe twenty-two, of medium height, on the thin side with a flawless, roseate complexion and two fluffy throw pillows for lips. A cascade of straight strawberry-blond hair fell diagonally across his forehead like a surfer boy.

I studied him carefully for a few moments, then, for some stupid reason, tipped my hand. "See anything you like?" I shouted out the window. I had meant it in a playful way, but it came out shrill like my mother calling me in for dinner. Startled, he looked up with those dreamy aquamarine-flecked eyes and took off.

But like clockwork, he returned to his usual spot the next morning dragging on a fag and following my every move like an apprentice artist watching Michelangelo outline *The Last Judgment*. Though I would have denied it if anyone ever tried to call me on it, the fact that my spy was a total babe brought out the latent exhibitionist in me. Instead of overalls I now wore tight denim cut-offs (that nearly cut off my circulation) and a torn wifebeater (made the tear myself).

My fey Stanley Kowalski routine, however, was completely lost on Viktor, who waved to me as he emerged from his parents' apartment.

"Do you have a moment, please?" he said softly. "I see you are fixing? You have plans?"

There was something about his tone that I found grating, so I decided to equivocate. "Just want to get the space in shape in case I need to rent it." *Not that it's any business of yours.*

Viktor nodded and bit his lower lip. "Ah, good. But if you

would be so kind," he said, "my father, he is not well. Another bad night."

"I'm sorry to hear that. Your mother certainly makes no bones about telling me when we make too much noise. But I'll alert the workmen to clear any future hammering or sawing with her."

Of late, Martina and I had come to some sort of détente. She was still as much of a pill as ever and not one to shrink from a confrontation—except with Olga. She was petrified of Olga. But once she had spoken her peace, she'd retreat and rant at Peter for a while for all the good it did. I'm sure he tuned her out years ago, situational deafness being one of the hallmarks of any successful long-term union.

"Most kind," Viktor said, bowing slightly and backing away from me like an obsequious servant in the Raj.

"When he is feeling better, perhaps I take him to my home for a few days, so you are free to work." He reached in his wallet and handed me his business card. Viktor, it turned out, was a dentist. Big hands for a dentist, I thought. "But please to give me advance notice so I can discuss with wife." I'd love to meet Viktor's wife if for no other reason than to swap horror stories about Martina.

I promised to take Viktor up on his offer, and he tipped his hat and walked away. Then I waved to my voyeur, performed an impromptu soft shoe on the uneven cobblestones, and climbed back up the ladder, wiggling my behind. I thought I heard him titter, but it was probably just my imagination.

The highlight of the following week was the university's presentation of Bertolucci's *The Conformist*. As soon as it was announced, I ordered Olga to clear her social calendar and instructed Nina to call in sick at work. Even though the available print was a somewhat blanched-out 16 mm, it couldn't completely dilute the film's awesome beauty and power. Afterward, my gal pals waxed poetic about the risqué tango between Stefania Sandrelli and Dominique Sanda. They were thrilled, this being the first time they'd seen same-sex attraction depicted onscreen.

The rest of the movie, however, hardly qualifies as gay rights manifesto, which in my current situation had a sobering effect, giving rise to a nagging sense of presentiment that lingered over the next several days. Was I conflating the protagonist with my personal spy? Would it come back to haunt me? My only peccadilloes were matchmaking two young women who might never have demonstrated the *cojones* to declare their love and wanting to open a place where gay people might congregate without shame or fear. Otherwise, I'd been the perfect overseas visitor.

The plan to open a gay coffee house in this repressed cranny of Eastern Europe was still a well-kept secret confined to a small band of Olga's sympathetic friends at university, who she swore were as trustworthy as they were discreet. Nina remained skeptical, however, and I was beginning to agree with her. Given the duplicity of self-hating homosexuals, it was conceivable that one of Olga's college buddies might have blown the whistle, and my spy was gathering intel until the authorities had gathered enough evidence to arrest me.

Even Nina's groom had begun asking questions, though she claimed it had mainly to do with his sense of entitlement. She was now a married lady and I was a single male, and a foreigner at that. The time we spent together fixing up the café might engender gossip and bring shame on Ralf's illustrious family. Nina assured him that I was smitten with Olga and she was helping out only because I'd promised her a position in the coffee house. But the questions persisted, and I wondered if we'd underestimated Ralf, especially after the way he'd glowered at Olga on the day of the wedding. He might be lying in wait for the perfect moment to spring his trap, exacting revenge on his unfaithful wife and on me for engineering the betrayal.

Ralf's displeasure only added to my sense of impending doom. The paranoia fed on itself, and I suddenly wished Caroline were here to slap me back to sanity. "What you're experiencing, Matthew, is guilt, pure and simple. You ran out on your life and now you're expecting to be punished for it."

But Caroline was not here, so my angst continued unabated—not helped at all by the fact that one morning, my secret agent vanished.

Thank goodness Olga had just completed translating the fourth notebook, the perfect distraction.

NOTEBOOK FOUR (1946)

After disembarking in Bremen one blustery, overcast day, Isaac sets off immediately for the various displaced person camps and refugee centers the Allies have set up since the signing of the Armistice. He is hoping to locate any surviving family members or, failing that, at least be apprised of their fate. Every town he passes through has been partially destroyed and is in utter chaos. It is as if during the war, the laws of gravity were suspended and the buildings carelessly hurtled into one another and burst into flames, leaving behind only rubble and ash and a populace wandering about in a stupor, sifting through the detritus for proof of their former existence.

Isaac's fluency in English ingratiates him

to the Americans and British personnel who operate a majority of the repatriation facilities. They offer to make inquiries on his behalf in exchange for his help in communicating with their charges. Trying to extract information from these spectral beings has been difficult and, in many instances, fruitless, the administrators contend. They seem to have forgotten the simplest details of their lives, and what little they can recall is disconnected and illogical.

But when Isaac queries them, he discovers it is quite the opposite. The men and women he speaks to remember everything about their infernal descent; it's as indelibly etched on their brains as the tattoos on their forearms. Though they survived the ordeal, they find no solace in it. Over the next several weeks, Isaac learns of treatment so barbaric and without mercy, he can hardly believe it was perpetrated by fellow human beings. Even for war, the depth of cruelty seems bottomless.

When he returns to his hotel in the evenings, his head is bursting with the gruesome accounts he's heard during the day. He lies awake all night side by side with the ghosts of the living and the dead and, at times, fears he may lose hold of his sanity. Rest comes only after he makes a solemn vow to remember the story of every troubled soul he has met on his journey and repeat it to anyone willing to listen. Only by bearing witness can he somehow hope to lighten their burden, a token gesture of communion from one who was spared.

In the search for his family, the information Isaac receives is either inconclusive or completely erroneous, leading him around in circles. Come back in six months, maybe a year, he is advised, then we will have more accurate records. For the present, however, the primary mission is to help the refugees get back home or start a new life elsewhere.

If it can be called good fortune, a few weeks into this expedition, Isaac runs across a familiar face purely by accident. At the front gate of yet another relocation facility, he is stopped so that a motorcade can enter. The cars and jeeps hold military personnel. From their strong open faces and crisp uniforms, he recognizes them as Americans. One high-ranking officer catches his eye, though he cannot immediately place him.

The man bestows a confident smile on Isaac along with a familiar wave of the hand. Of course, Isaac says, it's the Allied commander, a man with such charisma that it's easy to understand why his soldiers placed their trust in him and followed him into battle. Isaac acknowledges that without this man's efforts, he might not be standing here today and most of the people he has spoken to would have perished with the rest.

Isaac follows the procession as it wends its way into the camp. He is directed to the inquiries office where, as he pores over the camp roster, the general enters and the room snaps to attention. The commander salutes them, then offers his hand to anyone who will take it. Isaac eagerly grasps the general's hand. He mouths a respectful "Thank you," but is uncertain whether the general heard him. Distracted, he loses his place on the camp roster and completely misses his family name.

As he is preparing to leave, a clerk asks for a favor. Would he serve as translator to an elderly woman who has sores on her arms and legs and is refusing medical treatment? Isaac agrees. He is impressed that the woman maintains an almost aristocratic demeanor despite her physical debilitation. She confides that she has a small but painful growth at the base of her spine but is afraid to tell the doctors. They might decide she is too old and frail to continue and have her eliminated. Isaac assures the woman no harm will come to her, but she is obdurate. Though he is initially torn as to whether he should confide the woman's secret, he decides to relay the information to one of the doctors, who thanks him and promises to be discreet.

When he stops by to bid the woman farewell, a man halfway across the camp shouts out his name. Isaac is a common enough name, he thinks, and does not turn around. But the caller persists. When Isaac finally glances over, he notices a stooped over old gentleman in the distance repeating his name over and over again and assumes he is not in his right mind.

The man stumbles toward him in small, unsteady steps. "It's your uncle Moritz," the man cries out. "Why do you continue to ignore me, you disrespectful boy?

Isaac shakes his head. Not possible.

Uncle Moritz was a portly man with voracious appetites—good food, wine, and the kind of women deemed unsuitable by his long-suffering mother, who despaired that her brother would ever take a wife and carry on the family name. The gaunt, hunched man standing before him bears not a shred of resemblance to that jocular bon vivant. Isaac turns away, but the man clamps his wrist with his skeletal fingers. Have I changed so completely that you do not know your mother, Lotte's, brother?

It is with Moritz that Isaac's search for his family comes to an end. After taking the quaking man into his arms, Isaac's racing heart almost stops when his uncle whispers, "Oh my boy. Of us all, only we two remain." His worst fears realized, Isaac lets go a stream of tears and deprecations the likes of which he never would have believed himself capable, as if, now that the truth has been revealed, words have lost all meaning and value, and he can hurtle them through space like grenades, without concern as to where they might land. It is only when Moritz implores him, please, do not punish me for being the bearer of these awful tidings, that Isaac takes pity on him and regains his composure.

I want to know everything, uncle, he says. Are you strong enough? Moritz asks. Isaac suddenly feels foolish. Forgive me, dear uncle, I am behaving like a child. Unexpectedly, Moritz begins to chortle, his rib cage rattling in amusement. Isaac expresses concern, as if the movement might cause the bones to separate and his uncle to collapse into a heap, which only makes Moritz laugh all the harder.

My boy, you are truly comical. You know that my dear mother, your beloved grandmother, used to tell people that the reason I was so large was because I had big bones. As we can see, this is clearly not the case. I must thank you, Isaac. Because of you, I am laughing. I thought I'd completely forgotten how. Of course you are behaving like a child, my sister Lotte's child. That is to be expected. It is who you are and always will be in my eyes. No matter what age you achieve or how successful you become in life, you will forever be the little boy I once bounced on my knee. I'm sure your mother, may she rest in peace, would feel the same if she were here. Now come, sit with me and I will tell you what I know.

Despite his frailty, Moritz's mind is as sharp as it was in the days when he used to calculate prices for his lumber customers in his head, accurate to the penny. He shares the details with Isaac, sparing him nothing. Isaac vows he will not lose his temper again or worse, tumble into despair, if only for his uncle's sake.

The circle in which Isaac was raised and nurtured is no more, his uncle tells him. But save your tears. They are of no help and won't undo what has been done. Our very existence, yours and mine, and that of your sister in America, must be the family's vindication. Despite the Reich's best efforts, we have not all been eradicated.

His dear mother Lotte was the first to fall,

shot in the back when she tripped along the route of the forced march to the train station. Your mother did not suffer, Moritz assures him, and was at least spared the indignities that followed. Isaac's sister, Mina, already a sickly and distracted girl, was further weakened by hunger and contracted dysentery during the first winter in the camp. Her light was extinguished in a matter of days, another perverse blessing, Moritz assures Isaac.

As for Meyer, Isaac's father, an oak of a man with a will to match, he, along with several other men in the camp whose wives and children had perished, decided to end his own life by starving himself. He would donate his meager daily rations to younger men to help them survive. Given the harshness of the winter and the backbreaking labor, Meyer expired within a month. I was there beside him, still living off the fat I had accumulated in my salad days, and I showed him the shiv I had fashioned to slash my own throat if they forced me to take the gas.

On every stop along the way, Isaac had heard similar stories. By comparison, the fate suffered by his parents and sister was relatively merciful. And for that he is thankful, though he is still pierced through with feelings of horror and guilt and loneliness. Isaac chokes on the idea that he and his sister were able to survive in comfort and companionship in a land of prosperity while the rest of their family was being systematically exterminated.

Isaac thanks Moritz for his candor and for

having endured such suffering. Tomorrow, I will come for you, uncle, he says, and we will return home. Moritz spits on the ground. That place is no longer my home. They turned their back on me and fed me to the wolves. It is a wound that will never heal.

Then where shall we go, uncle? We shall go nowhere, Moritz replies. You are now a citizen in a new world. And I hope that, wherever you go, you find only happiness. But these people are my family now, he says, sweeping his thin, elongated fingers in front of him.

I have met a woman who wants to go to Jerusalem, he confides to his nephew. He does not say it as a boast but rather with a sigh of gratitude. Isaac is touched to hear that, even in such fallow ground, love has insistently bloomed. But uncle, he argues, the British will never let you enter.

Moritz shrugs. Moses was told he would never reach the promised land either and yet, he persevered. If I only get to see it from a distance or am able to touch my feet on the ground for a moment, I will be satisfied. Now go and live your life. And I will live mine.

A week later, Isaac is standing in front of the house where he was reared, viewing it through foreign eyes. In all his years abroad, he has often thought of this place and of the inhabitants of the neighborhood. He refuses to call it a ghetto, a word now fraught with calamity. There was Bela the grocer, who was so large he sidled like a giant crab and could only fit through the door of his shop by entering sideways. And Hannah, to whom he was dispatched on a weekly basis to drop off or retrieve an altered garment and, as a reward, received a peppermint candy from the gentle seamstress who had three long hairs spouting from her chin.

Looking around him now, it is as though he has invented these people. Or worse, that he had taken a wrong turn somewhere and is now in a completely different town that only seems familiar. What other explanation is there for these streets, once thick with activity, where conversations were conducted with passersby from upper-floor windows, but are now silent, a silence so absolute that not even the remembrance of past sounds can be evoked?

Doors have been torn off their hinges and there is not an unbroken window pane to be found. The building façades are smeared with obscenities, the defiled rooms stripped bare. Not even the tatters of curtains adorn the window frames to help conceal their nakedness. Isaac wonders if any of the other residents survived and whether, after he left, others were fortunate enough to escape, their pockets crammed with money scraped together by family and friends who selected them to be exempted from the coming annihilation. If so, he hopes those chosen few will return as he has and join with him in trying to rebuild the neighborhood in memory of the men and women who helped deliver them from the madness yet were powerless to save themselves.

He enters his building and climbs the three flights of stairs and walks through the family apartment searching for a trace of his former life. The thick oak doors and cornices, the crushingly heavy antique dressers and armoires, even some of the floorboards, have been removed, no doubt for use as firewood during the years of wartime deprivation and the long, bitterly cold winters. He does not condemn the looters. After all, what use do ghosts have for such fineries?

From the living room window he glances out over the roofs at the city beyond the empty shell of his neighborhood, a town that is gradually awakening from a troubled sleep to find itself occupied by the Soviets, who promise them a more equitable future, whether they want it or not. He says a brief prayer. He has never been a religious man and, after the events of the war, is even less inclined to believe in divine benevolence. He prays simply because he doesn't know what else to do.

He includes Tonio in his invocation, since Isaac has no proof that his friend still walks these streets. As they had agreed before he set out for America, Isaac was not to write lest his letters be traced. The few messages he received from Tonio ceased soon after war was declared. In Isaac's suitcase is a bound sheaf of correspondence he wrote to Tonio during his stay abroad. He has also brought back jazz records and a rendition of the popular song "I'll Be Seeing You," a shamelessly maudlin paean that he nonetheless listened to countless times.

Isaac considered enlisting soon after Pearl Harbor, but his sister reminded him that he had been sent to America to guarantee his survival. To place himself in danger would go against the family's wishes. Also, she stressed, he officially did not exist. He was someone named Tonio, and his true identity was known only to a select few relatives and their friends who would do everything in their power to ensure that he remain a secret. When the war was over, they would proudly parade him as a miracle, a small miracle of their own making.

During his sojourn in America, Isaac had poured all his energies into work, always finding a willing employer through the same loyal network of relations and friends who zealously protected him. Should anyone outside the circle inquire as to why such a healthy young man was not in the military, a letter was prepared by the family physician, Dr. Mastrov. It discussed ongoing treatments for a rare blood disorder. There was also a superbly forged backup document signed by no less than a U.S. congressman.

Isaac rarely spent a penny of his earnings, hoarding the money in the anticipation of helping his family begin anew after the war. He refused to even consider that they might all perish despite increasingly grim reports to the contrary.

A portion of his savings was earmarked for

Tonio, the man responsible for saving his life and whose seeming betrayal Isaac had carefully orchestrated to provide his friend with an alibi once the theft of his passport came to light. It troubled him that, after all these years, Tonio had no way of knowing whether their plan had succeeded or if Isaac had been intercepted en route and returned to the same troubled cauldron as the other members of his family.

He stubbornly refuses to even consider that Tonio might also be a casualty. In his mind, Isaac envisions the moment when they will again be face-to-face, which inevitably reduces him to sobbing. Then he remembers that Tonio had always frowned on such emotional demonstrations and, for that reason, Isaac took great care that his letters be devoid of florid drama. To do so, he had to recast Tonio as merely a fictitious pen pal to whom he was imparting information about of his life abroad.

For the most part, the letters are a diary highlighting the sights he and Tonio had talked about seeing together someday. He wrote of the majesty of standing on the observation deck of the Empire State Building, the exhilaration of watching jitterbug contests at the Savoy Ballroom in Harlem, of the hot, muggy summer Sunday afternoons spent sitting under a striped umbrella at Jones Beach. In reading over the letters, however, he notes that he was not always dispassionate and objective. His true feelings sometimes bled off the page no matter how carefully he worded them. But nothing was to be done. His pen could not be contained, as if it was in control and not the hand that guided it.

Having paid his respects to his family and neighbors, Isaac can no longer postpone his search for Tonio. He races down the stairs and jumps on a nearby trolley to the other end of town. Why does it move so slowly, he wonders. He can run faster than this, which is what he eventually does.

He arrives winded at Tonio's doorstep. Glancing up at the third-floor flat, he sees that it too has been forsaken. The floor-to-ceiling windows are no longer swathed in rich brocade. The balcony, once cluttered with greenery, is now empty and forlorn. He stares up at it for such a long time that he arouses the concierge's curiosity. The large young woman, a cigarette dangling from her lower lip, emerges from behind the lace curtains at her station and asks, what is your business here, sir? I am looking for the family of Mr. Edvard, the noted city official, he tells the woman. And who might I say is inquiring? A childhood friend of Edvard's son, Tonio. I was a frequent guest in their home. The former concierge would remember me. Katrina was her name.

The young woman takes a last drag on her cigarette. She crushes it underfoot and says, Katrina was my mother. She is dead, beaten with the butt of a German rifle until her brains spilled out right there on the sidewalk not two feet from where I stood watching, simply for talking back to the bastards. You probably recall that she was a woman who did not suffer fools.

I am so sorry, Isaac says, realizing that he has still not lost the capacity to be shocked.

Mr. Edvard, the woman continues, is also dead. After the Russians pushed out the Germans, the people turned on the mayor and dragged him through the streets tied to the back of a car. Mr. Edvard dispatched his wife and daughter to the country to live with relatives. He was found two days later hanging from the chandelier in his dining room but only because the ceiling plaster finally gave way from supporting his weight.

And Tonio, the son, my good friend? Do you know what has become of him?

He went off to fight. We heard that he had been killed in battle, she reports and her words slice through Isaac's calm exterior, and he has to steady himself against the wall of a nearby building. I can't swear to it, she continues, but one of the women in the building claims she saw him not three weeks ago at the central market. He appeared quite sallow and walked with a pronounced limp. When she introduced herself, however, he was the same gracious young man. He tipped his hat and presented his wife and child. She said he appeared to be in good spirits.

CHAPTER NINE
SEX AND SWASTIKAS

The brushed metal chairs I'd ordered from Poland were due for delivery that morning, so I got up extra early to make room for them in the café. Despite the frequent sops I'd been paying the workmen, the refurbishment had fallen behind schedule. They either arrived all at once and got in each other's way or disappeared en masse for days at a time. Still, the café's distinctly '50s retro ambience—powder-blue walls, pale gray flecked Formica table tops with chrome trim, black-and-white checkered linoleum—was coming together. Nathaniel would have been proud and amazed by my stick-to-it-iveness without a single meltdown or regret. Follow-through was never one of my virtues.

As I entered through the hallway, I noticed that the morning light, which normally floods through the plate-glass windows, was blocked. As I moved closer I saw why. The façade of the café had been defaced with a giant swastika. When I ran outside, I saw that underneath the Nazi insignia were two words scrawled in giant letters, one of which I recognized as "Jew." The other was unfamiliar, but my hunch was that it didn't mean "welcome."

Curiously, my first reaction wasn't sickening violation but *How did they know I was Jewish? I mean, I barely know I'm Jewish.* My émigré grandparents died when I was very young, and my folks were so assimilated they thought pastrami on rye with Gulden's mustard was too spicy. Except for the usual Yiddishisms that are part of most New Yorkers' vocabulary, I have only a vague affinity to my roots. I'd been to Reform temple exactly twice in my life, once for Ben's bar mitzvah and the other to attend the wedding of one of my coworkers.

When I turned thirteen, my parents were already divorced and the subject of my bar mitzvah was never broached. If you tortured me, I couldn't tell you the difference between Purim and Passover. Well, perhaps that's an overstatement. I mean, I've seen *The Ten Commandments* at least a dozen times, mainly for the camp value and all those buff, shirtless men. So I know all about the lamb's blood on the door. As for Purim, I got a crash course when one of my male students sauntered into class on a bright spring day dressed as Queen Esther. Gender can be very fluid in seven-year-olds. Otherwise, the high holy days signified only one thing to me: no classes.

I've had plenty of gay slurs cast at me, especially during my stay at Willow Ridge. But prior to that morning, my closest personal encounter with anti-Semitism had been an account in the *Daily News* about some hoodlums defiling tombstones in a Jewish cemetery on the Queens/Long Island border a few miles from my house.

Fear, however, soon overtook me. And when I'm frightened, I tend to freak. And when I freak, I lash out at anything or anyone in my path, starting with Martina, who chose this opportune moment to return from her morning grocery run. Surveying the scrawl, she grinned smugly as she slipped through the front door. I gave her an earful and, for good measure, kicked the front door a few times.

My next victim was this year's winner of the "Mr. Aryan Youth" contest, who had returned—coincidence?—and was enjoying a smoke under the archway. "So, is this your doing or maybe your buddies over at the KGB or Stasi or whatever goddamned secret fraternity you pledged?"

He just stood there and took my abuse with such a convincingly wounded look on his face that I felt like a bully. I was too keyed up to stop now, however, and I actually challenged him to a fight, raising my fists and dancing around like a boxer, although the effect was more Rockette than Rocky Balboa. But he didn't take the bait. Instead, he fell back and did a slow fade down the alley.

Later, as Olga, Nina, and Alexei surveyed the damage, a woman who lived across the way told Olga that while giving her baby its midnight feeding, she'd been standing at the window and noticed a couple of thugs running off after spray-painting the storefront.

"You see?" Olga said. "Just some ruffians blowing off steam." She reassured me that her parents had seen much worse during the Soviet era. And I reminded her that a similar boys-will-be-boys explanation was offered after Kristallnacht. But both she and Nina downplayed the incident. At least they didn't attack me physically, they pointed out, which did not console me one friggin' bit.

I was only half-kidding when I asked Alexei if he might locate the perpetrators and see if they could be bought off. He actually stroked his chin and took it under consideration. Then, big surprise, he said he knew just the man to remove the spray paint. I was assured that within a day or two, the front of the café would look like new. For a price, of course.

We all agreed that reporting the incident to the police would be a hollow gesture and would give rise to more questions than we were prepared to answer. Foreign visas can be revoked on the slightest pretext. And given the cops' lax attitude toward the rabble-rousers and their tendency to blame the victim, it was perhaps best not to involve them.

For the rest of the day, I holed up in my room licking my wounds and sucking on a bottle of ice-cold vodka. I had to talk myself out of booking the next flight home.

Now, I don't want you to think I'm a yellowbelly. I conquered most of those demons back at Willow Ridge, where I learned that if someone calls you a sissy and you bust his nose, that pretty much takes care of the problem. Even bullies are loath to face the ignominy of being beat up by a fairy twice. Most of them were merely experiencing the usual homosexual panic, and if there's one thing I do understand it's homosexual panic, especially in adolescence. Besides, we're all messed up about sex in some way; it's such an unruly urge. Caroline told me that one of her ex-boyfriends confided that he never masturbated because he considered playing with yourself as gay. And he was one of her well-adjusted beaus.

But this was something else. The defacing seemed to confirm my recent sense of foreboding. Maybe this was another sign. *Time to go home, buddy. The café is almost finished. Let Olga and Nina take over from here.*

Which only made me feel like more of a wuss. I hate feeling like a wuss. It's so wussy.

In the midst of this push-pull argument, the doorbell rang. Probably Alexei, who had wasted no time hunting down the graffiti exterminator. Without thinking, I bounded down the stairs. When I opened the door there was no one on the other side. *Pranksters again? Neo-Nazis looking to up the stakes by doing some serious bodily damage? Shut the door, Matt. Quick. Shut the door.*

As I did I noticed a very tasteful floral arrangement. A spectacular potted orchid lay at my feet, three large magenta sprigs in a black lacquered vase. There was a note attached.

Dearest Matthew,

We do not know each other, but I would never wish you harm. I must apologize for the actions of my countrymen, cowards that they are. I wish I had the courage to say this to you in person, but every time you are before me, I cannot speak.

With great affection,
Janusz

Janusz? Who did I know named Janusz? Then I peered across the way and there he was, my Secret Agent Man standing under the arch puffing away, batting his baby blues from behind a curl of smoke. Cocking my finger, I urged him forward. As he approached, he flicked his cigarette in that tough-guy way that made me quiver. I pulled him inside, backed him against the wall, and pressed all my weight against him.

"Finally," he whispered.

Stroking his smooth cheek, I carefully leaned in and kissed his trembling cushiony lips until all traces of nervousness melted away. Then I took him upstairs and we got naked.

❖

Discovering Janusz's true identity was the ideal palliative to my recent trauma, and all thoughts of scurrying back home vanished. Sex can be a powerful sedative.

But more importantly, Janusz served as my reentry point into the dicey world of intimacy. Over the course of our affair, I learned a great deal about the contrarian nature of desire. There were so many reasons we shouldn't have gotten involved, starting with Janusz's sometimes imperious demeanor. Twenty-two-year-olds can be awfully smug and often unremittingly self-righteous. But I forgave his implacability. It takes a bit of growing up before you appreciate that the world is painted in varying shades of gray. I was less tolerant of his dourness. If Janusz had a sense of humor, he kept it under wraps. And for me, the ability to laugh at oneself is right up there on the list of attractive traits in a mate. Without it, there's really no way forward.

But since Janusz was a total cupcake with butter cream icing on top, I put on the blinders. For a time, I even found his behavior endearing. I particularly enjoyed the way he'd greet me at the front door with an officious handshake like he was priming a pump, march up to the apartment, sit on the edge of the bed, and unlace his short hiking boots with one claw-like tug, turn to me and say in a sober tone of voice, "May we have the sex now, please?"

Got me going every time.

I was Janusz's first, which was almost a relief for me since technically I was kind of a newbie myself. For the past eight years, I'd only been with one man. "Steam Room Walter" didn't count. That was merely self-gratification with an assist. And I had other insecurities as well. If I didn't drive Janusz absolutely wild, I'd feel doubly inadequate, like I'd lost my touch.

Fortunately, Janusz was a fast and eager learner, and we experienced only a brief period of adjustment. The first couple of times he had little staying power, which was understandable, though to his credit he had a remarkably short recovery time. He was also a tad graceless. However, once he'd grasped the rudiments, he began to appreciate the male body's other pleasure centers besides the obvious one. He also soon corrected his pacing problem and understood that while the occasional hundred-yard dash can be dandy, the real joy comes from being a marathon runner.

During intimate moments, he could be disarmingly unguarded. After one memorable workout, when I praised him for his standout performance, he blushed, he actually blushed. "It is because I do not want you to grow tired of me," he confessed with adoring eyes.

As if.

Now, this might sound strange, especially after listening to me wax on about his flawless looks, but I don't usually go for pretty boys. They're too symmetrical and manicured to get my mojo working. Janusz's saving grace was his earthiness, an intoxicating loamy aroma about him that offset his perfections. Outward appearance may beguile but the nose, well, it knows. Sexual chemistry is really nothing more than basic biology.

After lingering for hours in my arms, Janusz would reluctantly sneak back home to study for the rest of the night (he was completing his thesis for an advanced degree in political science with plans for a career in the foreign service), leaving me alone in my narrow bed to wrestle with my guilt.

C'mon. You had to know there'd be guilt. Not because I was allowing Janusz free rein of my body, but because for the first time since Nathaniel, I was experiencing an emotional connection.

Janusz cracked my hard shell of mourning and allowed welcome sensations of warmth to seep through. And to me, that smacked of betrayal. On several occasions, I fell asleep begging Nathaniel for forgiveness.

Then, one night in a dream, he gave me the all-clear. Nathaniel didn't actually put in an appearance, but it was clearly his doing. In the dream, I had just picked up a hero at Subway, but instead of going straight home, I dropped by Billy Wilder's apartment in Los Angeles to borrow a Miró.

Billy's a noted collector, and I'd seen the apartment and some of the art in a magazine spread a while back. I remember being especially impressed by the Miró.

This had to be a message from Nathaniel, there was no other explanation. You see, Billy Wilder, along with his respective collaborators Charles Brackett and I.A.L. Diamond, is responsible for three of the greatest last lines in movie history, one of which Nathaniel used on me whenever I got into a funk.

No, it wasn't "I'm ready for my close-up" from *Sunset Blvd.* Let's be serious. Nobody's ever really ready for their close-up.

And it wasn't "Nobody's perfect" from *Some Like It Hot* either, though I certainly gave him cause to trot that one out.

No, every time I sank into an orgy of self-pity, Nathaniel would grab me by the chin, look me straight in the eye, and say, "Matthew. Shut up and deal," from *The Apartment*—only the way he meant it had nothing to do with gin rummy.

Great advice, worked like a charm every time.

The dream confirmed that, in his own cryptic fashion, Nathaniel was giving me permission to pursue Janusz. Admittedly, it was stretch. I even jumped to the illogical assumption that he purposely sent Janusz to me—what you might call a Nathaniel *ex machina*. He'd always said he would do anything to make me happy. Why let a minor inconvenience like death get in the way?

Not that my guilt subsided completely, but for the most part I shut up and dealt with it. Still, I doubt that I would have been so cavalier about the affair if it hadn't come with an expiration date. Ours was the definition of a summer romance. I was due back at school right after Labor Day and, upon completion of his thesis, Janusz had been promised an overseas posting. A fling with built-in boundaries seemed the ideal way to inch myself back into the dating world. Janusz was like lover's rehab, an emotional halfway house.

Then, one night, as I was drifting off in his arms, Janusz said, "I must tell you something. And you must not laugh. I am falling in love with you."

That threw my spine into spasm. Before I could object, he placed an index finger on my lips. "Please. I do not expect you to feel the same. But you must understand. I have a need to be in love. If I am behaving the fool, please permit me."

I felt duty-bound to caution Janusz about falling in love willy-nilly. "That's how perfectly good hearts get broken beyond repair," I advised him.

"But I have lived all these years hoping for the good fortune to have my heart broken," he said with a rueful sigh. "To love a man has been my great desire, even if he does not return my affection."

If he wasn't worried about romantic shrapnel, well then damn the torpedoes. Besides, like losing one's virginity, heartache is a time-honored rite of passage.

After sneaking over to see me and then sneaking back home on a nightly basis, I was surprised when Janusz asked me to go away with him for a few days. "And you'll be comfortable being seen with me in public?" I asked.

"Not in front of my family or my friends," he admitted. "But it is necessary to teach myself to have courage so I may prepare for my life to come."

Janusz talked a good game, but I bet that if anyone asked, he'd palm me off as a visiting American for whom he'd been hired as a tour guide. Again, I gave him a wide berth. As with Olga and Nina, I recognized that the coming-out process was different in a culture where being even slightly unconventional is discouraged and downright dangerous.

Leaving Olga and Alexei in charge of renovations for a

few days, we hopped into Janusz's ancient Fiat 600, which he'd found abandoned on the side of a road and he and his brother had restored. The mental picture of him covered in axle grease made me break into a sweat.

I knew exactly where we should go, up the coast to explore the fishing villages where Isaac and Tonio had stolen away more than half a century earlier.

Along the way, we stopped at the great northern forest where the oaks and spruces were so tightly clumped they blocked out all the sound and much of the light. How easy it would be to wander into these woods and never find your way out again, a real-life Grimm's fairy tale. Janusz said he frequently came here and wailed his lungs out whenever he was trying to reconcile his nature or suffering from unslaked desire. The physical release, he contended, buoyed his spirits. When I told him about "primal scream" therapy, he grimaced. Janusz regarded any form of psychotherapy as the indulgence of spoiled Americans.

"Freud, Adler, and Jung would be so happy to hear you dismiss their lives' work as some kind of fad for bored capitalists," I said.

Janusz conceded the point but urged me to give the yelling cure a try. He would wait in the car in case I got scream-shy. Though I'm usually more of an imploder than an exploder, I roared myself hoarse that day. And he was right. Afterward, I felt oddly reinvigorated.

As we skirted the coastline, the chilly wind in our faces, I wondered out loud how such a babe had never scored before. "With that face, you must have been approached on a regular basis—by girls, guys, even the legally blind."

The very idea made him bristle. "You think I would give my affection to a person who was attracted to me for my appearance?" he scolded. "My face is only an accident of birth. It tells you nothing of my true nature. That is what will endure after I grow older. Any person who is drawn to me solely for my appearance will tire and move on to someone younger and more attractive. I am certain you did not respond to me for that reason."

"Well, your looks didn't hurt," I admitted. "You're a knockout kid, and you know it."

"I thank you for the compliment and I will say that I too found you appealing in a physical manner. But that is not what ultimately drew us together. It was mystery, a curiosity about the other."

"Yeah, I thought you were KGB and planned to turn me in and have me tortured, and not in a fun way."

"Do not speak foolishness. The KGB is outlawed here now. What I was meaning to say was that after the initial attraction, you were interested in my character."

"You give me too much credit. I can be as shallow as the next capitalist pig."

"I do not believe you. When you speak of your Nathaniel, you never mention his physical characteristics."

"Nathaniel was intensely beautiful. He had this inner glow that…"

"Ah, you see. You just confirmed what I have said. He glowed from the inside, just as you do. You can see why I was so frightened to speak to you. No, frightened is the wrong word. I must improve my vocabulary."

I suggested "intimidated" and he snapped it up. "Exactly. All I could do was admire you from a distance. But when you approached, I would run off because I felt insufficient. You have no understanding of your power."

"You're exaggerating," I said, secretly flattered. "But do go on."

"What is most attractive is how at ease you are. Where I

come from, to be gay is to hide, to be concealed, to be ashamed and afraid. But you have no need for that. It is clear in how you present yourself."

"Am I that obvious?"

"Yes. But not in the way you think. Oh, how can I make you understand?" he fretted. "You see, there are men who are very tall. Some are uncomfortable with their height as if it is a flaw. They try to make themselves smaller by walking with a stoop. But others embrace it. They walk erect and make no excuses. When I first saw you, I thought, 'Oh, so it is possible to be comfortable with the way you are.' It was an intoxication."

Then he pulled his car over to a shady grove by the side of the road and started kissing me and undoing the buttons of my jeans.

As we drove through the villages along the coast, we discussed Uncle Leonard's notebooks. Although he found the stories interesting, he remained a doubting Thomas. "Perhaps your uncle merely had this lover in his mind and wrote of it as a way to make it more real for him," he posited.

"That's exactly what Nina said. I got news for you, buddy. Men have been doing it with each other since…Have you read Greek and Roman history? If there was no truth to what Uncle Leonard wrote, why was he in such a hurry to return and why did he agree to remain under the Soviet heel?"

"It could be because the pull of the motherland is very strong."

"Yeah, I can see how he might have yearned for the joys of totalitarianism."

"You are making a joke?"

"Yes, I am making a joke."

"Perhaps you are right. Since I have lived here my entire life, it is hard for me to conceive that a relationship between two men was possible in those days except in their minds. It is merely an opinion."

"There are moments when you can be very mature," I said with a smile. Without thinking, I leaned in to kiss him, which caused him to almost lose control of the wheel.

"You are not in your country. You must be more careful," he chided.

Even in summer, the coastal beaches were rocky and uninviting and most of the hamlets ramshackle and impoverished, not the idealized romantic getaway I'd envisioned. But later in the afternoon, we happened on a charming little town and decided to hole up in a local inn where we booked separate but adjoining rooms. After a lunch of the sweetest lobster I've ever tasted, and Janusz for dessert, we took a stroll along the pier, and I discovered that we weren't the only ones who had sought out the seaside for a tryst.

Seated on an old wooden bench overlooking the lapping waves was recent newlywed Ralf playing kissy-face with a waifish and very pregnant young woman. Ralf, who is normally as clumsy as Babe the Ox, was remarkably graceful and attentive to the young woman. Then they got up and glided right past us arm in arm, taking no notice. The triste-looking damsel had her head on Ralf's shoulder like some disenchanted Chekovian heroine. He stroked her hair and mumbled assurances. Who knew the big lug had a soft side?

Though I insisted that it was my duty as a loyal friend to tell Nina, Janusz forbade me. "This is not your concern," he said.

"But doesn't she have the right to know if her husband is two-timing her?" I argued.

"Very well," he conceded, "but then you must also tell Ralf about his wife and Olga."

"That's different," I snapped. "For one thing, he seems to have gotten this woman pregnant. Nina can't get Olga pregnant."

Pretty lame, I admit. And Janusz thought so too. He said I was jumping to conclusions, which led to our first fight and, later, glorious make-up sex.

I made a mental note: Argue with Janusz more often.

Turns out I didn't have to tell Nina about Ralf. Small towns have big ears. Upon his return, Nina confronted Ralf with his perfidy and negotiated strict terms for a truce—think Joseph Stalin at Yalta. He was free to see the girl, whose name was Sonia, but in return Nina demanded the child to raise as her own. I was as taken aback by her demands as Ralf must have been. But Nina later explained to me that she and Olga had always intended to have children using Ralf as their sperm donor. The fortuitous pregnancy would save her the rigors of labor and poor Sonia the shame of a bastard child.

If Ralf refused, she promised to parade her wronged wife story all over town. Women in this society might be second-class citizens, but they do have certain inalienable nagging rights. Nina wasn't trying to be vindictive or heartless, she reassured her hapless husband. Sonia, with whom she had been acquainted since grade school, would still be the child's mother and could visit whenever she pleased. But the baby would live with them and be raised as their own.

As it turns out, Ralf's inamorata was not averse to the idea. She too was about to enter an arranged marriage with a man who lived several towns away and she rarely saw, so her parents were overjoyed by Nina's face-saving proposal. They even offered Ralf a small monthly stipend to take the child off their hands.

I confess to being rather amused at being a supporting player in this evolving Eastern European soap opera. But

Janusz was outraged. "I do not understand your friends. How can they live with such dishonesty?"

"You're right. Let's go tell your parents how much fun we had after you tied my wrists to the bedpost last night."

That shut him up but good.

Thus far, I'd kept Janusz to myself, but I couldn't avoid introducing him to Nina and Olga indefinitely. I tried to convince myself that they would hit it off. They shared a common heritage, a similar sexual persuasion, and Olga and Janusz attended the same university.

I could not have been more wrong.

First off, there was a class barrier. Janusz hailed from a prosperous upper-middle-class family. Olga and Nina resided on a much lower social rung. The baby/infidelity drama had already poisoned his perception of them as Aryan trash and, to top it off, he was a bit of a chauvinist as well and uncomfortable with the dynamics of female-on-female sexual attraction.

I accused him of being a snob and a misogynist, which did no good. He saw it as a badge of honor, his *droit de seigneur*.

Olga and Nina proved to be equally inhospitable. The ever-wary Nina still regarded him as a spy. I assured Janusz she would eventually come around. She didn't like me at first either.

But Nina was positively cordial compared to Olga. When Janusz and I returned home from a day trip, we found her sitting at my kitchen table chipping away at a new notebook. Foolishly, I left them alone while I went out and shopped for dinner. They were having a nice enough chat when I left, discussing their experiences at university and their future plans. While I was away, though, the conversation took an unforeseen detour when Janusz, with the best intentions I'm sure, suggested that she might want to tamp down the butch routine if she hoped to secure a teaching position at the university.

Well, you can imagine how that went over. Olga railed at him, said he was both a homophobe and a prig, and in the process, inadvertently blurted out my real reason for opening the café.

Oops.

I had deliberately avoided the subject with Janusz. Given his daily trips out of and back into the closet, it was best not to push my luck. I merely said that the café was a memorial to Uncle Leonard but did not elaborate.

As I walked in, Olga and Janusz were jabbing at one another from opposite corners of the apartment. When I tried to referee the dispute, they turned on me.

"How can you give yourself to this Judas?" Olga fumed. "Nina is right. He thinks he is superior, when he is merely bourgeois."

"And you, do not know your place as a woman," Janusz lashed out at her.

Yup, that's what he said. Those exact words.

Olga lunged at him and grabbed him by the throat. "I am more of a man than you," she said. And then for good measure, she added, "Pussy."

I should never have taught her that word.

After I pulled her off him, Janusz barked, "And what about your American friend who is so willing to put us all in danger?"

"Whoa, whoa, whoa. Let's not go crazy here. It's a coffee house, not a bordello," I protested, for all the good it did me.

"It was not his idea, it was mine," Olga boasted.

"Then you are just as demented," Janusz said, those beautiful lips frothing.

"What do you suggest? That we remain hidden and ashamed forever?" Olga parried. Then she stormed out of the room. But not before calling him a pussy again.

After a stern but benevolent lecture about his unenlightened attitude, Janusz tentatively apologized. But not about the café. "What if some harm should come to you?" he fretted. "I would be inconsolable."

When he got all frothy and apoplectic, there was only one sure way to calm down Janusz. Afterward, while he smoked one of his wretched-smelling filterless cigarettes, I mentioned that while I was touched by his concern, I was quite capable of handling myself.

"You have no idea what you are saying," he told me, but at the moment I was too high on my horse to pay him any mind. I reminded him that he also owed Olga an apology. Initially, he balked. Then I informed him that if he ever hoped to be successful in the foreign service, it might be helpful to begin by practicing diplomacy at home.

He eventually conceded, but not about the café, which he maintained was a cockamamie idea and a potentially dangerous one. So I had to distract him again.

Men are so easily distracted.

Despite his disapproval, Janusz was in attendance the day the café sign arrived. He agreed to attend the lighting ceremony after I conceded that his stubbornness didn't hold a candle to my bullheadedness. Workmen spent most of the afternoon securing the neon Cinemascope masterpiece above the entrance while an electrician finished installing the special wiring to juice it. That night, just after dusk, Janusz, Olga, Nina, and a chastened Ralf stood beside me as Alexei flipped the switch.

We were not prepared for how vivid the sign would be in its full glory. "So American," Janusz said as he shaded his eyes, "big and ostentatious."

"Yes. Three cheers for the red, white, and blue," I countered, offering up a toast with a glass of the best mediocre bubbly I could find. Later I asked Alexei if he could take the glare down a notch. Olga translated. "He say nothing to be done. The only way is if European war was won by general with not such a long name."

After most of the others had left, Olga, who had begrudgingly accepted his tepid apology, helped us finish off a second bottle of the cheap champagne, fully aware that we were courting major hangovers. Olga gave us a preview of the fifth notebook, and we all reflected on Isaac and Tonio's touching efforts to keep their love alive, which made our problems seem inconsequential indeed.

The broad strokes of the next chapter were accompanied by the glorious *Au Fond du Temple Saint*, after which Olga leapt up and proclaimed, "I know what we must do. We must tell Peter about what your uncle has written. It is our duty."

On the face of it, her argument held merit, though inebriation tends to give rise to dubious notions that would otherwise never take flight. I believe that's how the rueful phrase "it seemed like a good idea at the time" was coined, probably by the captain of the *Titanic* who, after one absinthe too many, announced, "Iceberg, schmeisberg, I'm going to break that transatlantic speed record."

And we all know what smashing success that was.

"But if what your uncle wrote is true, then Peter already knows," Janusz opined.

"Yes, is possible. But he does not know that we know," Olga argued.

As if to prove I can be as addle-brained as the next person, I added, "You're absolutely right, and while we're at it, we should tell him we're reopening the café."

Janusz groaned and repeatedly slapped his forehead. But Olga and I were already too infected by our brilliance to pay him any mind.

"I know just when we're going to do it," I continued, undeterred. "Right after Martina goes out grocery shopping tomorrow morning."

"We will not sleep tonight, so we are prepared," Olga suggested, which also in the moment seemed like a brilliant stroke. Spirits should come with a warning: *Never drink and think at the same time.*

Janusz rose and stumbled to the doorway. "You can do as you wish, but I will not take part in this lunatic behavior."

"Then go to your home. No one asked for your help," Olga growled.

"Come on, children. Play nice."

I offered to walk with Janusz but only after making Olga promise she would not under any circumstances surrender to Morpheus while I was gone.

It was a balmy night for this part of the world, what they call a heat wave and I call short-sleeve weather. Both of us were feeling no pain, and we fell into a rough-and-tumble encounter in a dark alley around the corner from his house. Janusz, amused by his boldness, giggled all the way to his front door, tickled that he had tapped into his inner bad boy.

On my way back, I wondered what would become of Janusz after I returned to Long Island and sincerely hoped I wasn't falling for him.

When I got in, Olga was passed out in a chair, mouth hanging open, drool cascading down her chin. It took a good half hour to revive her, pouring coffee down her gullet so we could put the finishing touches on our farrago.

Next morning, at ten on the dot, Martina embarked on her daily grocery run. Like superheroes, we sprang into action. I whipped out my giant key ring as we tiptoed down the stairs and let ourselves into the apartment where Peter was quietly napping in his chair. He stirred as we approached. He was even frailer than the last time I'd seen him. His eyes flashed fear and disorientation, his head twitching from side to side as if trying to assess whether we were really standing there or merely an hallucination.

"We are here to bring you wonderful news, old man," Olga said in a soothing voice. "This man, Matejus, he is Leonard's great-nephew."

No reaction, just a tremulous, open-mouthed gaze.

She held up one of the black marble notebooks and showed him the first page. "Do you recognize the writing?" He twitched slightly and put his hand to his chest. In a few brief sentences, Olga laid out the story and Peter's eyes widened.

"Do not be afraid," she tried to reassure him. "These stories are a great tribute to your friendship." Peter put his hand to his mouth and I was starting to think we'd make a terrible mistake.

"Matthew. Go. Open the door. Let him see the café," Olga commanded. As I pushed open the entrance and turned on the light, a yelp caught in Peter's throat. His eyes went glassy as if he had fallen into a trance.

"I don't like this, Olga. Let's get out of here. Martina's due back any minute."

Olga put her face up to Peter's and beamed. "Be happy, old man," she said, shaking the notebook in his face. "Your story will be told."

Peter froze. Not so much as a blink.

"Come on, Olga, let's go," I said, grabbing her hand. "Now."

We tiptoed out and pulled the double doors shut. Olga started climbing the stairs when I heard a rap at the café door. Odd, I thought. I wasn't expecting any workmen. As I walked through the café, I noticed two policemen standing in front.

"Matthew Robins?" I nodded. One of the cops started

nattering at me, and I held up my hand. "Sorry, no *capisce*," I said and called out for Olga.

Then he whipped me around, handcuffed me, and took me away.

NOTEBOOK FIVE (1948)

After a few discreet inquiries, Isaac finally locates Tonio's residence and place of employment, and then carefully avoids them. Whenever he is in the general vicinity, he takes the added precaution of altering his appearance, wearing a long coat, year-round, and a wide-brimmed hat pulled down around his face, and dark glasses—a rather comical disguise, like Bob Hope in one of those silly wartime spy comedies Isaac so enjoyed when he went out to the movies during his years in America.

One morning, as he emerges from the bank, he hears someone call his name. While the voice is not Tonio's, he nonetheless picks up his pace. He cannot be too careful, he tells himself. At the end of the street, he disappears into an apothecary where, to kill time, he improvises several imaginary ailments. The shop is empty and the chemist is only too happy to listen. A half hour later, Isaac thanks the man for his guidance, purchases a packet of lozenges, and is on his way.

The possibility of running into Tonio is a source of constant anxiety. Isaac is torn between his desire for them to be reunited and the likelihood that it would further complicate their lives. He briefly considers moving to another town, or perhaps even returning to the U.S. But he has not waited all these years only to be separated from Tonio for good. Even if they cannot see one another, it is enough to know Tonio is nearby and that if his friend is ever in need, he will be able to come to his aid.

And for a time, he takes consolation in that.

Isaac has found himself a secluded apartment on a cul-de-sac in a sparsely populated neighborhood behind the university, on the opposite side of town from where Tonio resides. His days are spent tutoring young men and women in Russian and English. Despite his innate timidity, he finds he is quite at ease with his charges, and his enthusiasm as a teacher proves to be infectious. His pupils are eager to recommend him and soon Isaac's services are in such demand, he must occasionally turn new students away. Yet, though his days are quite busy, Tonio is never far from his thoughts: It is six p.m. Is Tonio enjoying dinner with his family? Does his son idolize him? Does his wife treat him with respect? Does she make sure he lacks for nothing? Does he love her? Have his wife and son completely supplanted his affection for me?

In his quest to quiet such rumblings, he returns to university, where he is now welcome, to complete his degree. He briefly considers marrying, but there is, understandably, a shortage of available single Jewish women, and the few who managed to escape the genocide have largely resettled elsewhere. He is forced to concede that if he was serious about marriage, he would somehow find a bride. But such a union would be contrary to his nature, and it would be wrong to burden the life of some innocent young woman.

No, he must live for Tonio and content himself with that. In all the years they have been separated, he has given into his yearnings with only one other man, a chance meeting on the way home from university late one desolate winter evening. The encounter left him at odds with himself. This is not who I am, he concluded. My affections cannot be randomly transferred from one person to another. I've no choice but to be faithful to the dictates of my heart even if there is no possibility of reciprocation. He accepts the hardship, knowing that to do otherwise would be a betrayal of his feelings and he would be left with less than nothing. Isaac must remind himself of this promise from time to time, particularly on the days when loneliness is perched on his windowsill and refuses to be silenced or fly away.

Isaac would probably have continued in this manner had it not been for Tonio's determination to locate him. From the moment Isaac stepped off the boat in Bremen, despite a lack of tangible evidence, Tonio became convinced that he had returned. It was as if he'd suddenly developed an inexplicable telepathy. Now, almost daily, he imagines that he sees Isaac, or rather familiar fragments of him: the familiar V-shaped rise of Isaac's shoulders in one man, the gait of his walk in another. He hears Isaac's unmistakable chortle behind him and turns expecting to find him standing there. Each disappointment only serves to make him more resolute. His sightings have to be more than coincidence, he insists. Isaac must be nearby, just out of reach.

But what if Isaac has indeed returned and has no intention of seeing him again? Perhaps his feelings have altered in the decade since they dedicated themselves to one another. After all, they are now grown men, not young boys caught up in an infatuation. So much has transpired in the interim that a change of heart would be completely understandable, if nonetheless untenable. Still, if he could only be sure Isaac was safe, it would settle his mind. Then he could mourn the passing of their affection and treat it with the same deep sense of loss we reserve for the few special beings who enter and, sometimes prematurely, depart our lives. Tonio has survived the war and now he will survive this as well, he concludes. But first, he requires proof that Isaac has come to no harm, while at the same time acknowledging that if his great friend has perished, his own life would lose all its meaning.

Just as Isaac eventually tracked down Tonio by making a few polite inquiries, once his friend sets out to find him, it is but a question of time. His efforts eventually bear fruit through a polite inquiry made to a mutual friend who teaches at the university. He is pleased to learn that Isaac is currently finishing his studies and surprised to hear that he returned two years earlier, right after the armistice. It is of no consequence, Tonio tries to convince himself. All that matters is that Isaac is alive and his heart is beating close enough that he can almost hear it.

However, the day soon arrives when the idea that his friend is nearby and just out of reach is insufficient. So he doggedly pursues Isaac right to his apartment door. Standing there, he takes a few moments to steady his nerves. When he knocks, the sound of Isaac's voice from within is startling and an involuntary sob escapes him. Then Isaac opens the door, not tentatively like someone uncertain of who is on the other side, but with abandon, as if he knew full well that it was Tonio and had been anticipating and dreading that rap every day since his return.

For Isaac, the shock is almost unbearable. Instead of surging forward to embrace Tonio, he stumbles back, a look of terror on his face. He crumples to the floor like a penitent. Tonio enters and extends his hand. "My dear Isaac," he says with a smile, as if they'd just run into each other casually on the street, "are you not pleased to see me?"

Isaac lowers his chin to his chest, which heaves so wildly that he must place a hand over it to keep his heart from bursting through. For a moment Tonio is sorry that he surprised Isaac in this manner. Perhaps he should have written a letter and allowed Isaac to decide when—or even if—they should meet again. But Isaac might have refused or, worse, not responded, and he could not have endured that. No, regardless of the outcome, he had to see him again.

Isaac takes a moment to calm himself before rising to his feet. "Forgive me. I had so convinced myself we would never meet again, that for a moment I was afraid it might be true."

Tonio cradles Isaac's hand, and they exchange polite kisses on each cheek. They refrain from even a fraternal embrace, which would have been appropriate since they'd been separated for almost a decade, an irretrievable decade. But somehow they sense that were they to take hold of one another, they might never let go.

Isaac offers Tonio a seat and prepares some tea. As it steeps, he takes down a suitcase from above the armoire and retrieves the letters he wrote to Tonio. "I already know a great deal about what has happened to you. This will tell you about my life while we were apart. I want you to know everything. Read them. I will go out and get us something to eat."

Tonio races through the letters as if they might be taken away from him at any moment. He is struck by how many similar thoughts and sentiments they shared over the years and across the continents. By the end of the evening, which runs very late, their convivial rapport has returned as if they'd never been apart. The ease with which they resume their friendship is at once exhilarating and intimidating. Nothing has changed and yet again so much has.

"We must make time to see each other every day without fail, even if it's just in passing," Tonio says as he reluctantly rises to depart.

"I am at your disposal," Isaac responds and, after Tonio departs, he circles the chair in which he'd been sitting and replays every single moment of the evening since he first heard the knock at his door.

CHAPTER TEN
OH BROTHER

When we talk about fate, we tend to be very specific, favoring the positive: falling in love, or receiving an unexpected inheritance. But an untoward occurrence such as the premature death of a lover or being incarcerated in a foreign county—well, we prefer to view that as happenstance, arbitrary.

Twelve days in an airless, windowless cell cannot be accurately counted out in coffee spoons. But it does give you time for contemplation and reflection, perhaps too much. If I were a convinced criminal—which, thankfully, I was not yet— given the choice between life imprisonment and execution, I'd favor a fast exit every time. It would be infinitely preferable to spending years, decades even, confined to a cement cubby hole with toilet en suite often in the company of a roommate almost guaranteed to be aggressive and/or hostile and/or amoral and/or mentally unhinged. *Hear that, warden? I'll have the lethal cocktail, please. No ice.*

Over the first few days of enforced solitude, I sought to amuse myself with time-wasters like compiling top ten lists of favorite songs, broken down by genre: rock, R&B, jazz, the great American songbook. Next I catalogued the movie tapes and books I would take to a desert island, or in this case a Siberian gulag.

In between, I slept a great deal. Still, by the seventh day I was flirting with stir-crazy, chewing my fingernails down to the stump. Sorry, Nathaniel. "Shut up and deal" was not going to get me through this predicament.

After almost two weeks, I still had no idea why I'd been arrested and had pretty much given up hope of an arraignment given that I was in the land of guilty until proven otherwise. My demands to see Lawyer Bombyk were met with blank stares by the guards, whose dour dispositions appeared to be a prerequisite for the position.

I was permitted a weekly shower, which for a daily bather like myself is a shock to the olfactory system, and the less said about the grime-caked porcelain god in the corner of my cell, the better. Otherwise, conditions were downright tolerable. The two daily meals were oddly tasty, obviously homemade by some unseen angel of mercy, and comforting. On alternate days, a guard accompanied me to an inner courtyard where I was permitted a fifteen-minute *passeggiata*. I harbored no fear of molestation. The guards were far too lethargic and, except for the guy in the opposite cell who remained curled up in a fetal position the entire time, the joint was empty, a testament to the Soviet era's crime-deterrence programs. People had obviously gotten out of the habit of breaking the law during their occupation. See? Even totalitarianism has an upside.

Solitary confinement allowed me the luxury of constructing elaborate conspiracy theories involving everyone from the devoted Olga and Nina to the "I think I'm falling in love with you" Janusz. Had my gal pals been setting me up since the start? Was Janusz actually a government plant, willing to throw in his body in order to gather evidence against me? As day and night blended together, my circadian rhythms devolved into chaos, and paranoid Cold War notions of intrigue bubbled to the surface with myself as the protagonist in a game of international political muscle flexing.

My biggest fear was that by the time Caroline—the only person in the known universe who might conceivably miss me—tried to track me down, I might already have been moved to an undisclosed location. At any moment, I expected someone to drop a cloth bag over my head and to spirit me away in the middle of the night and sell me into white slavery probably to some oleaginous Middle Eastern pooh-bah or Mongolian warlord. I tried to imagine what I'd look like in a harem outfit. *Do these balloon pants make my ass look fat?*

As reality slipped beyond my grasp, I had this *Manchurian Candidate*-like delusion that my brother Ben was sitting across from me in a black pinstripe suit, an attaché case across his lap, grinning that crooked grin of his. Panicked, I bolted upright and screamed at the phantom to go away and leave me be. Then I closed my eyes tightly and counted to ten. But when I opened them again, he was still there, that sickening simper even wider.

"How's it hanging, dude?" The wraith spoke. "I didn't want to wake you 'cause you're obviously in need of a good night's sleep. You look like shit, man."

For a few moments I entertained the possibility that my miserable wretch of a brother might actually be sitting in the cell beside me. No, impossible. The only way you'd ever get Ben off the island of Manhattan was extradition.

"Our landsmen treating you well?" he asked in that unnerving way Ben has of turning a solicitous question into an insult. "Sorry I took so long getting here. I had one major headache to iron out at the office, and, as you know, it takes several light-years to get to this part of the Milky Way even on the *Millennium Falcon*."

Tentatively, I confronted the ectoplasm. "If you're really Ben, how did you know where to find me?"

"This woman Caroline called me. Said somebody phoned her long distance late one night and said you were in the hoosegow and, long story short, here I am. Boy, you really stepped in it this time, kiddo." He chortled.

Now that's the Ben I remember. Always eager to jab a dirty finger into a gaping sore. "That you find this amusing really says a great deal about you," I huffed.

"Hey, I'm not the one who decided to open a business in Outer Slobovia. What goes on in that fevered little brain of yours?"

"Why? Is it against the law here to be an entrepreneur?"

"No, but the way you went about it definitely is," he said, tipping his straight-back chair on its hind legs, savoring the moment.

"So what are the charges against me?"

According to Ben, I'd been cited for bribing public officials, which Alexei had claimed was mandatory, and ignoring several statutes pertaining to foreigners legally operating a going concern.

"So as a foreigner, I'm not allowed to open a café?"

"That's not what I said. There are just some really arcane permits and licenses that have to be pulled. And the riffraff that was helping you out, well, let's just say they bribed all the wrong people. Lucky for you the laws here are very much in flux, and the current climate favors anyone who wants to contribute to growing the local economy, even damned Yankees."

Ben stood up and brushed off his jacket. "But more later. Right now, I'm still jet-lagged, and I have an appointment later with your pal Mr. Bombyk who, as I'm sure you already know, is a total *putz*, though in his defense, he hasn't been completely useless." He tapped his briefcase against the metal bars to get the guard's attention. "Sit tight, bro. I should have you out on bail in a couple of days."

"Why not right now?"

"Because Bombyk and I still have to finish drawing up the papers to satisfy all of the requirements for foreign business ownership—which you will then have to sign."

"And the bribes?"

"They dropped the charges." Ben clanged on the bars again.

"How did you get them to agree to that?"

"Simple. I paid off the *right* people this time. In greenbacks. You should have seen their greedy eyes light up at the sight of dead presidents. By the by, you owe me five grand. But I'm not going to charge you interest, blood."

"You've got to stop trying to talk like a rapper. It diminishes you."

"Oh and one more thing. How do you manage to sleep in that army cot of a bed, and can you tell me why such a small apartment has such a big bathroom?"

"You got into the house?"

"The front door lock was wide open, and there's not a soul around, upstairs or down. It's a wonder nothing was stolen."

But robbery was the furthest thing from my mind. If the house was abandoned, it could only mean one thing. Peter was dead.

❖

On the walk back home from the jailhouse, Ben lagged a few paces behind, which took me all the way back to kindergarten, when Mom forced him to accompany me to and from school every day.

"I'm not a child, you know," I snapped.

"Jury's still out on that," he said and, as if to prove there really is such a thing as karma, put his foot down wrong on a slippery cobblestone and almost turned an ankle. "How the hell are you supposed to walk on these goddamn streets?"

"Maybe you should have left your Bruno Maglis at home."

"Be nice."

"This *is* me being nice."

The front door lock of the house had been pried open and was dangling limply like a puppet on its day off. As we entered, Martina emerged from her apartment carrying a package neatly wrapped in butcher paper.

"Martina. I am so sorry to hear about Peter," I said, hoping she'd at least pick up on the sympathetic tone of my voice.

Instead she slapped me across the face and marched out the door.

"Whoa!" said Ben. "What'd you do to her?"

"I think she thinks I killed her husband."

"Let's hope not. I don't practice criminal law."

Over dinner, as Ben inhaled my home-cooked stew, I laid out the details of Uncle Leonard's saga. When I told him about the love affair with the recently deceased Peter, Ben waved me off just as Janusz and Nina had done. I was embellishing, reading between the lines. I didn't understand the complexities of male friendship because I insisted on seeing the world through "a gay prism."

The subtext was unmistakable: Gay men can't be trusted to have a wider grasp of reality because, unlike straight dudes, we only think with our groins. I would have walked out if I'd had any place else to go.

When I related the details of the graffiti incident, however, I had his full attention.

"Sonofabitch," he said, talking with his mouth full.

"Ah, finally, a hate crime you can relate to," I snapped.

For the rest of the evening, he fulminated about the alleged attack. I pointed out that "alleged" implied that I'd made it all up and actually spray-painted the place myself in an attempt to garner sympathy. "Besides, I'm opening a gay café, not a B'nai Brith." I snorted, immediately wishing I could eat my words.

"A what?" Ben said, and proceeded to tear into me, accusing me of having lost my few remaining marbles. "Why are you deliberately trying to provoke these people?" he yelled. "I can just imagine what Nathaniel would say if he was here."

"You have no idea what he would say, asshole. And you're not allowed to talk about Nathaniel. You gave up that privilege after you punched him in the face because you found out we were fucking."

Normally, I'm careful to edit out four-letter words as they travel from brain to mouth, a process I'd mastered by working around seven-year-olds all day long. But there's something about Ben that brings out the latent longshoreman in me.

"See, this is exactly why our relationship deteriorated," he said.

"I got news for you, buttmunch. Something that never existed can't deteriorate. Relationship implies more than just sharing space or being dipped in the same gene pool."

"What an ungrateful little shit you are," Ben fumed. "If it wasn't for me, you never would have met Nathaniel."

To prove to Ben how much I'd matured, I covered my ears with the heels of my hands and started stomping my feet. "Stop saying his name," I said through gritted teeth, "or I'm going to scream."

Our little tiff might have escalated had we not been interrupted by Nina calling out to me from the bottom of the stairs. When I went down to meet her, she made the sign of the cross and hugged me. "I'm okay, Nina, I'm okay," I assured her. She grabbed my hand and pulled me toward the door. "Olga," she said in an ominous tone two registers lower than her normal voice.

"Where are you off to now?" Ben called down.

"I'm not sure. Don't wait up."

"Okay, blood," he said.

"Stop doing that!" I yelled.

But Ben merely shrugged, humoring me. "Excellent stew, by the way. When did you learn to cook?" he said before waddling back into the apartment.

Nina jumped behind the wheel of Ralf's sickly-yellow clunker. Using hand signals, I said "I didn't know you could drive," which so distracted her she lost control of the wheel and almost plowed into a lamppost.

"What's wrong with Olga?" I asked, and when I saw tears stream down her face, I took it as a bad sign.

The city's main clinic was as crammed as Macy's on Black Friday, and every bit as chaotic. Gurneys of untreated patients and their families littered the hallways. How could the city jail be so empty and the hospital packed so tight? Nina led me to a small ward at the end of the corridor and pointed to the far corner where an almost unrecognizable Olga was sitting up, her swollen face various shades of black and purple, her left arm in a sling nestled against her bosom. She was attempting to sip ice water through gargantuan lips, and when she saw me, she spilled the entire glass.

"Jesus Christ. Who did this to you?"

Before Olga could respond, Nina blurted out "Alexei" and launched into a litany of my favorite local swear words. Why is it that profanities are the first thing we learn in a foreign language and the last thing we forget?

Olga struggled to get her mouth working, but the words

dribbled out one at a time. How frustrating for a motormouth like Olga to have her words muted and stifled. "I go to police to help you. Alexei say no. I say yes, and we fight." She heaved a sob and snot gushed from her nose.

"Where is the bastard?" I asked. Olga pointed at the opposite wall, and I peeked around the corner. Alexei was stretched out and barely conscious, his jaw wired shut. It was a classic case of "You think I look bad? You should see the other guy."

"That's quite a right hook you have there, missy!" I complimented her. Olga nodded and, as evidence, offered up her broken hand. "I hit him. Then Nina, she throw him down stairs."

"He is," and here again Olga gathered all her strength to finish her thought, "a pussy."

"Pussy," Nina agreed.

They were totally hooked on that word.

Olga pushed out her already swollen lower lip, and giant baby-doll tears rolled down her face. "Oh Matthew, I am bad friend."

Puzzled, I looked over to Nina and noticed that familiar look of censure in her eyes. Slowly, the story came out. I'd been hoodwinked by Alexei with Olga as his willing accomplice. They'd devised a foolproof plan to separate the guileless American from his inheritance, justifying themselves that I would never miss the money since I'd never expected to receive it.

"Americans have so much, they do not need," Olga said, though she sensed from my increasingly cool demeanor that she was skating on a thin-iced pond.

The workmen Alexei hired were mostly friends with only varying degrees of proficiency. Only the graffiti eradicator had been an actual pro. Most of the bribe money had gone right into Alexei and Olga's pockets. The city inspectors were real enough, though they too had been coached beforehand to pad their fees, with Alexei and Olga getting a taste.

Nina had been in the dark about all this and only began to suspect when Olga drove up one day on a new (albeit used) bike. Olga was evasive about where she'd gotten the money to buy it, but Nina pressed her. Woe to the woman on the receiving end of Nina's grilling. The KGB are greenhorns by comparison. Olga finally blabbed and Nina had a meltdown. She could not possibly love a common thief, much less someone who would betray a friend. She demanded that Olga immediately go to confession and that she and Alexei make restitution. Like Ralf before her, Olga immediately caved to her demands. She knew better than to bargain with a woman who claims to have Tatar blood in her veins.

"Nina is right," Olga cried. "I am shit. I can only say I am sorry. I do not expect forgiveness."

"Good," I said, still a bit stunned. "The only reason I might even consider giving you a pass is because someone beat the living crap out of you before I could."

"Yes, I deserve. But you must believe. I am not this kind of person. I become crazy. I am never so close to money before."

"Did you ever think that, instead of stealing it from me, you might have asked me to buy you a new bike?"

Olga seemed genuinely taken aback. "They do this in America?"

"Yeah, they do, but now I wouldn't treat you to a cup of coffee and a doughnut."

"What is doughnut?"

The curious thing is that, even though her betrayal smarted, I'd already partially forgiven Olga. All along I'd suspected that she and Alex might be skimming. In a way she was right. I'd practically painted a bull's-eye on my wallet and was then shocked, you hear me, shocked, that I'd been scammed.

Absolution is a funny thing. There are friends, even blood relations who, if they put one foot out of place, are immediately cut off. Disinherited. Banished. Then there are others you can't stay mad at no matter how serious the infraction. There's likely a sound psychological explanation for this.

True, Olga only came clean after Nina threatened her. While I might never really trust her again, greed is an all-too-human failing, and I still believed that at heart she was a good egg. After all, she tried to go to the cops and even took a beating for me. That indicates some nascent moral fiber.

Yet it seemed that ever since Olga came up with the idea for the café, one thing after another had gone wrong. I'm sufficiently Jewish that I would never ask the loaded question "what else could happen?" though I had a sinking feeling my troubles weren't over yet.

I did my best to conceal my sense of unease at least in front of Ben, but only because I didn't want to give him the satisfaction. To my surprise, he took my side when I told him about Olga. "Wow, and she was supposed to be your best friend. And then they call us ugly Americans." It felt so good that someone had my back, even if it was my so-called brother. I declared a truce and treated him to a guided tour of the city, expounding on the little history I'd picked up during my stay. He actually enjoyed it.

"Just think," he mused as we stood in the train station. "If our peeps hadn't emigrated, we might have grown up here instead of Hempstead," he observed.

"If our peeps hadn't emigrated, they would have been gassed, and we wouldn't exist."

"You got me there," he said with a slight quiver. "Hey, let's go buy me a bed."

Since there were no Sealy or Serta mattress shops in town, we settled on a sleeping bag. Ben preferred it to what he called "Baby Bear's crib" in which his size twelve feet flopped over the edge, the sight of which was undeniably precious. Mercifully, he didn't snore like Janusz. That boy has a major pair of adenoids.

Ah, Janusz. Another bitter reminder of the bollix I'd made of my Eastern European expedition. I still had no idea if he'd played any part in my arrest, or even if his affection had been sincere. To be fair, he'd warned me, and I just shined him on. But if he wasn't to blame, then why had he not shown his face?

Over dinner at the Café au Poivre, I formally introduced Ben to Nina, "the only one of my local friends to whom I am speaking at the moment and the only one whose moral compass is not totally askew." To which Ben countered, "You mean the Nina who's cheating on her husband with a woman and has dibs on his love child?"

"The very same, you prick." It dawned on me that Ben was enjoying himself, misconstruing our backhanded volleys for fraternal repartee, which might explain the succession of passive-aggressive bitches he dated. He would hardly be the first man, gay or straight, to mistake sniper fire for intimacy.

Ben curled up in his sleeping bag and immediately fell into a peaceful slumber with the contented look of a sheepdog clutching a large soup bone. Like Nathaniel, my brother is one of those "lights out" people who conk out the moment their heads hit the pillow. How I envy them. It takes me at least twenty minutes to negotiate my way to dreamland, and if somebody three houses down walks across a creaky floor, I'm up until dawn.

I was about halfway there when Ben suddenly jolted awake and yelled, "What was that?"

"Nothing," I moaned, "you're having a bad dream."

Then we heard a loud crash and Ben was out the door like a shot. I found him inside the café growling at two skinhead types who were in the process of trashing the place—swiping dishes off the counter, upending furniture and tossing a table through the front window. When I flicked on the light, they arched their backs like cornered rats. One of them spewed out one of the cruder epithets for homosexual.

"What'd he say?" asked Ben.

"He called me a degenerate," I responded.

Then the second intruder began hurling invective.

"What?" Ben asked.

"Yeah. I think you were included in that one," I said. "Something to the effect of 'dirty, filthy kike.' I'm paraphrasing, mind you."

"He actually called me a dirty kike?" Ben said, incredulous.

"Technically it was closer to 'disgusting heeb' or 'subhuman Christ-killer.' But that was the general drift."

Ben lifted off the ground like he had springs in his feet and tackled the guy. They rolled around on the floor barroom-brawl style, landing alternating punches. You didn't need a Foley artist to hear jaws crunch and nose bridges collapse.

The second goon set his sights on me. I picked up a chair and tried to keep him at bay, but he wrestled it away from me. I grabbed another and beamed him on the side of the head. As he was massaging the bump, I jumped on his back and wrapped my arms around his neck, which was as thick as a three-pound cabbage. He bucked and threw me off. I landed on my back and got the wind knocked out of me, but managed to roll away before he could pin me down. As I was getting to my feet, I saw this enormous fist coming at me in slow motion. A split second before my *shaina punim* was mashed to pulp, an unseen hand swatted it away.

My savior was Viktor and, when the goon saw him, he ran to the other side of the room and tried to make himself invisible. Viktor lifted the other guy off Ben by the scruff and dangled him midair. Only then did I realize that our fearsome intruders were merely overgrown boys.

"Who are these guys?" I asked.

"This one," he said referring to the one under his thumb, "I am ashamed to say is my son, Mikhail."

I quickly made the connection with Martina's pride and joy who had come by that day in the jeep to pick up his grandparents.

"The other," he spit out, "is his delinquent friend, Yuri."

"Did you know your skinhead son and his buddy vandalized this place a few weeks ago and probably denounced me to the police? If my brother, Ben hadn't come all the way from New York to rescue me, I'd still be in jail."

Viktor was apparently ignorant of these incidents. He lashed into his son, who crumbled under the assault and was unable to offer more than a weak denial. Then Viktor turned to his son's cohort, who was busy studying his shoes. Yuri stuttered a response and pointed to Mikhail. Viktor grabbed Mikhail's head and slammed it into the wall, one, two, three times. Ben mouthed an "ouch!" and I almost felt bad for the guy. Truly, there are few things in life more humiliating than having your old man clean your clock in public.

Mikhail slid down the wall, fighting back tears.

Viktor shook his head. "You think they are skinheads because of how they dress? Do not be fooled. They are both still sucking at their mothers' teats. I take responsibility. I have spoiled him. And Yuri. His father will know everything. I am sorry for your troubles. If police come again, please to call me."

"You have pull with the authorities?" I said, impressed.

"Yes. I do the teeth," he said, tapping his pearly whites, "for the chief of police and his family."

Viktor then fished a card out of his wallet. "This man, my cousin. He come tomorrow. Fix everything. You pay nothing."

"Thank you, Viktor. I was so sorry to hear about your father. I hope the end was peaceful."

Viktor nodded. "You are most kind. Father was ready. Without uncle, he not want to live. They are so close for so long. Last year, papa he almost die. We take him to hospital. Uncle come to say good-bye and the sadness too much for him. His heart stop on the way home. We make sure he have proper burial. He deserve for all he do for my family."

I asked Viktor where Uncle Leonard was buried. I wanted to pay my respects and to thank him for all he'd unknowingly done for me. If there had been any doubt in my mind about the affection between Uncle Leonard and Peter, Viktor removed it. He spoke without judgment in his voice as if he accepted the "friendship" as a fact of life, whatever his personal feelings may have been.

"My father is in same cemetery. Now they can see each other every day," Viktor said. He shooed Mikhail and Yuri out of the café. Some of the neighbors who had gathered outside yelled at them. One woman spat on the ground at Mikhail's feet.

"So we are good?" Viktor said.

I nodded.

He looked over at Ben. "I am sorry to meet you under such circumstances."

"You should be." Ben grimaced. "If it was up to me, I'd put those little punks in jail. I don't appreciate being called a filthy kike."

Viktor covered his eyes with his hands. "Idiots. They don't even know what they are saying."

"I think they know exactly what they're saying," said Ben, clicking his sore jaw.

"I speak to him. He did not learn this from his father," said Viktor.

"Maybe his grandmother?" I offered. Viktor sucked his teeth but offered no rebuttal.

As they drove away, Ben started to laugh. "I gotta say, that was kind of fun."

"I'm so glad. I live to amuse you," I said, dabbing the blood from his upper lip with a dish towel. "You're going to look like a raccoon in the morning."

"And I was impressed at how you held your own. I always assumed you were a total limp wrist."

"Another stereotype shattered."

"Sorry they ruined all your hard work," said Ben, surveying the damage. "But maybe it's for the best."

"Nonsense. A minor setback. We're still opening two weeks from tonight," I said, shaking Viktor's cousin's business card at him.

"No way. You're getting your ass back to New York where the natives aren't so restless."

"You can go. But I have to do this, for Uncle Leonard and for Peter—and for Nathaniel."

"And I'm the sanctimonious one?" He sighed. "Okay, if that's what you want. I'll stick around just on the off chance you're charged with crimes against the state."

"Now who's being grandiose?" I said. But I was touched by his uncharacteristically noble gesture. "What about

Hungadunga, Hungadunga, Hungadunga, and McCormack?" One of the few things Ben and I have in common is an abiding passion for the Marx Brothers. "Won't the bloodsuckers miss you?"

"I got three weeks' vacation coming and like maybe six months' comp time. I could use a break. This place ain't Paris, that's for sure. But you know, it's kind of growing on me."

CHAPTER ELEVEN
CAFÉ EISENHOWER

As part of our reconciliation, Ben and I got into a jogging routine. Mostly he just tagged along behind me. I had to grant him props for stepping out of his comfort zone to rescue me, which likely had less to do with brotherly love than the promise he made to Mom to keep an eye on me. Despite all that garbage about the gay son being the mama's boy, Ben was the one who was always hanging from her apron strings. Her "little man" was also her closest confidant.

They were forever whispering and exchanging knowing glances. Mom doted on Ben, laughed at all his pathetic jokes, and they ran up ruinous phone bills after he went off to college. I don't mean to get all Tommy Smothers here, but Mom had little energy left over for me, especially after her health went into decline, though she felt guilty about it, which made me feel guilty. And that, friends, pretty much sums up our mother-son dynamic.

Somehow, Ben and I managed to remain civil to one another, which is not to say that I became immunized to his annoying habits: the way he tipped his chair on its rear legs and rocked back and forth; or the little symphony of belches after each meal; or his insistence on playing loud music whenever he was in the john so no one could hear him make. I once suggested the *1812 Overture*, which he did not appreciate. While he didn't snore, Ben occasionally whistled in his sleep, not a soft passage of air but a full-on toot, like he was one of the Three Stooges. How did this dude manage to keep a girlfriend for more than a week?

If pressed I suppose Ben could recite a litany of my faults as well, but hey, this is my story, not his. Besides, anyone who's read this far should be acutely aware of my shortcomings by now.

Even during as neutral an activity as jogging, he found ways to irritate me, starting with tedious warm-up stretches that even a certified marathon runner would have deemed ridiculous. Then there was the sweat, as if his cranium was an old showerhead spritzing in every direction. His pants and groans, which I might have found raw and sexy in another man, were tantamount to gay aversion therapy.

After our runs, we cooled down in silence on the banks of the river. One morning I happened to casually ask him (not true, it was totally calculated) about his latest Trudy-Mandy-Sandy girlfriend, whose name I'd completely erased.

"Over," he responded curtly.

"What happened?"

He offered no response.

"Could that be one of the reasons you're in no rush to get back?"

Again, tomblike silence.

"You know what I think?" I ventured.

Ben made the "T" sign. "Thanks. But I pay a shrink big bucks for his opinion."

"If you ever want to talk about it…"

"You would be the last person I would go to."

"Geez, you don't have to get persnickety about it."

"I'll tell you what. We'll talk all about my old girlfriends when you let me talk about Nathaniel. Deal?"

Grrr!

❖

Ben also joined me on movie nights and found another way to work my nerves by rapidly tapping his index finger against his lips as he watched the film. It took all my willpower to restrain myself from reaching out and snapping his finger like a string bean. His skewed opinions also got under my skin. He gave *Wages of Fear* a tepid review: too slow and it had subtitles and it was in black and white and when the nitro blew there was no big kaboom, just a muffled poof. "Not very cathartic," he noted. Ben much preferred the following night's showing, *The French Connection*—for the car chase, though he did grouse that the plot was difficult to follow.

"Just out of curiosity," I ventured, "what's your favorite movie?"

"That's easy. *Caddyshack*. Cracks me up every time."

"Wow. You're a regular Pauline Kael."

"Hey, I call 'em like I see 'em."

"What is it with you straight guys? The better educated you are, the more you feel you have to talk street?"

"Blah, blah, blah," he replied.

"Can I quote you on that?"

Nina and an almost fully healed Olga were in the audience for *The French Connection*. When she saw me come in, Olga crouched down hoping I wouldn't see her. Good luck with that. Figuring that she'd try to cut out early, I made a beeline for the exit.

"I'm still mad at you," I said with a scowl. "But that doesn't mean I've stopped caring about you."

"I don't deserve," she whimpered.

"Never mind the false modesty, how about a hug?"

She embraced me greedily, and I told her that the café was opening in six days and I wanted her to be there. And if she was still interested, I needed her to translate the final notebooks.

"I promise. And you do not have to pay me."

"Good. Cause I had no intention of doing so."

On the way home, Ben and I stopped at a pub for a quick one, and by closing time, we were pretty much three sheets apiece. We ambled over to my favorite river bridge, the only wooden one with its big, thick pillars embroidered with Rhineland mermaids and an imposing Poseidon. The boards creaked beneath our feet as we made our way to the center and peered down at the sludge-laden river, which seemed in no great hurry to move downstream. We must have stood there for a good half hour before Ben succumbed to the dipso-blues and got all boohoo on me.

"Uh, you okay?" I asked, mostly out of politeness. I was praying he'd get self-conscious and wave me off.

"I know you said I'm not allowed mention his name, but I miss Nathaniel so much," he bawled. "I really fucked things up, and it kills me that I can never put it right."

"If you're looking for sympathy, you're pissing up the wrong tree."

"This is not about you, okay? I screwed things up with Nathaniel long before you came into the picture. Didn't he tell you the reason we stopped being friends?"

"All he said was that you freaked out, I assume because he was gay."

"There's more to it than that. It was because of that douchebag Joel."

Nathaniel had told me about Joel, another of their college buddies, whom he technically seduced, though it was more a case of "boy, was I drunk last night."

"You think he took advantage of Joel? That not how I heard it."

"I could give less of a shit how it happened. It was what happened after."

"What? Did Joel freak out and try to slash his wrists?"

"You don't know? He went around bragging that he'd screwed Nathaniel, like he'd just won the Pulitzer Prize for sodomy."

"You have such a colorful way of expressing yourself. But if you don't mind my saying so, you sound just a teensy bit jealous here."

"You missed your calling, Matty." (I *hate* being called Matty). "It took Dr. Baranski a full year to get me to admit that. I mean really, all Nathaniel had to do was ask. I didn't even need to be drunk. Well, maybe a couple of drinks."

I screeched and grabbed my head in both hands. "You have to stop talking immediately."

"Look, the truth is nobody in our group, male or female, would have turned down the chance to sleep with Nathaniel. It had nothing to do with sex."

"Now I'm totally confused. First you turned on Nathaniel when he told you he was gay. Now you're saying you would have overlooked all that if he'd jumped your bones instead of Joel's?"

"Exactly. Look, I'm not gay but—"

"Why is there a *but* in that sentence?"

"I mean, I never had the hots for Nathaniel. But I loved him more than any other guy I knew. We were like this." Ben fused his index and middle finger.

"Really? Who was on top?"

"Look, I'm trying to discuss something very painful. Could you please stop being a jackass?"

"Sorry."

"I swear on Mom's grave, I never had any designs on Nathaniel and God knows I saw him naked enough, even with erections, when we were roommates."

"Please, I beg you, stop."

"Nathaniel and I were intimate in every way except sex. I told him things that, to this day, I've never shared with any of my girlfriends. And he told me things that, except for you, he probably never admitted to anyone either. I knew all his flaws and still I idealized him."

"Uh, still sounding pretty gay."

"It's taken years of analysis to sort this stuff out. So shut the fuck up and let me finish."

I held up my palm in surrender and suddenly felt light-headed. I stretched out on a bench to study the night sky, which was inky blue and stellar.

"Do you know why you fell in love with Nathaniel?" Ben asked.

"No, but I have a feeling you do."

"It's not because you're gay. You fell in love with him because everybody fell in love with him. And that's really what pissed me off."

"Whoa. That's taking sibling rivalry to a whole new level."

"Me? Why did you choose him out of all the guys in the world, if it wasn't to spite me?"

"That has to be one of the most egotistical things you've ever said. Did you know that because of you we almost didn't get together? You were like this invisible shield between us."

"I did not know that," he said, though I wasn't sure whether he was being empathetic or was curiously flattered.

"If you had slept with Nathaniel, I don't think either one of us would have been able to get past that. And I would have missed out on the best eight years of my life."

"If it's any consolation," Ben said, "I was more upset with him than I was with you. It was as if he'd broken a trust. Like he was a predator."

"I came on to him, Ben, not the other way around. So that's why you barged into our house in the middle of the night and attacked him? Wow. Now you've gone from creepy to full-out deranged."

"I did that for you," he said.

"How do you figure?"

"I somehow got it into my thick head that Nathaniel was putting you in danger. We all knew how much he slept around, and I thought he probably had AIDS and was going to infect you."

"How well could you have known Nathaniel, if you thought him capable of something like that?"

"I'm not saying he would do it deliberately. But this was in the early days, before they'd even identified the virus. If I'm guilty of anything, it's being overprotective."

This confirmed my theory that Ben was a total mama's boy. "Look," I said, "if it it's any consolation, Nathaniel and I never had unprotected sex, even after we'd been monogamous for several years. For one thing, it makes you last longer and—"

"No, no, no," he said, wagging his finger. "I'm glad you were happy together. I don't need to know how happy."

I could see that Ben was starting to sober up and that brick by brick, he was rebuilding his protective façade. "Just so you know, I think about pussy on the average of every fifteen minutes and have since the age of twelve. Day and night. I don't know how I ever get anything done. Besides, a guy's junk is gross. I feel bad asking women to put their mouths down there. And don't even get me started on body hair."

"That explains the airbrushed white girls you date. Okay, I let you talk about Nathaniel, now it's my turn."

Ben's shoulders caved, like he'd been benched right before the big game.

"So while you were in therapy did you come to any conclusion about why you can't hang on to a woman?"

"That one was easy. I'm a shitty boyfriend, a misogynist with anger issues. But hey, look at my primary male role model growing up. You're the only person in our family who's ever been in a successful relationship, though it was with Nathaniel. I mean, how hard could that have been?"

"What brought me to Nathaniel may have been what brought everyone to Nathaniel. What sustained us was his unconditional commitment. I gave him plenty of reasons to bail on me. But he accepted my neuroses as part of the package. He said I was the real deal, that I was genuine, even if I was sometimes a genuine pain in the ass. He was no god either. He was caught in a vicious circle of trying to please everyone, then buckling under the weight of their high expectations."

"Yeah, we discussed that," Ben interjected. "I told him it was much easier to be a bastard. Then if you do something nice, people are genuinely impressed."

As he spoke, Ben's voice grew increasingly faint. By the time he'd finished his thought, he was half a block away, waving over his shoulder. "I'm gonna take a walk. See you back home."

When I got in, however, Ben wasn't there. He didn't

return until after sunrise when, without a word, he slipped into the sleeping bag.

I stood over him, tapping my foot.

"What?" he said. "With all that sex talk, I needed to trim the horns."

"But where? How? Who?" I stuttered.

He rolled his caterpillar eyebrows and explained. Using his "straight-dar," Ben had found his way back to the narrow streets near the university, which he had previously noted were unusually busy for a town where, as he put it, "they roll up the sidewalks at sundown."

Ben assured me that he was not in the habit of paying for sex. He'd only done so once before on a business trip to New Orleans, "because if you're going to pay for it, New Orleans seemed like a logical place."

Even in his inebriated state, he said, he was disappointed that, up close, most of the available ladies were decidedly over the hill, garishly made up with chunky ankles. He was about to give up—"I was more lonely than horny," he confessed— when he happened upon a svelte little number clad in a trench coat and little else who "looked like Audrey Hepburn, only with tits." Her name was Konstantina. Tina for short.

"Well, I hope you had a good time with your whore, while I sat up all night worried sick that you were lying in a gutter somewhere with your throat slashed," I said with my usual flair for melodrama.

"I don't believe that for a second. But thanks anyway. I did have a great time. Twice." He placed a pillow over his head and was asleep in seconds, whistling contentedly like Curly.

❖

If only I'd met Viktor's cousin, Wassily, two months earlier. The man was a genius. He quickly repaired the damage and even made some significant improvements in the café. When he arrived, he scoffed at the inferior workmanship done by his predecessors. It made me almost grateful his nephew had thrashed the place. By the time Wassily was done, the café looked exactly as I'd envisioned it. The creamy yellow walls were decorated with the original Eisenhower artwork, which I'd cleaned and had reframed. The tables were speckled gray and white Formica with chrome chairs and pale blue padded vinyl seats, the floor was black-and-white linoleum tile, and the entire room was lit by bright fluorescent tubes.

Wassily's truck appeared one morning with a vintage jukebox in the back. The red-and-white neon music players still held some vintage 45s—really bad Soviet-era propaganda rock. But I didn't care. It was the perfect decorative focal point for the place. When I offered to pay him for it, he demurred, so I bought him a case of vodka, which he happily accepted. You can never go wrong with vodka around here. It's like currency.

The night before the official opening, as I walked around the darkened café, I sensed the presence of ghosts. Not the spooky kind, but happy spirits. Uncle Leonard and Peter reunited? Nathaniel? My mother, my grandmother? Old friends? Wishful thinking again, but hey, where's the harm in that?

I'd decided on July 29 for the official kick-off because it was Uncle Leonard's birthday. That morning, Ben and I visited his grave, which is in the cordoned-off Jewish section of the town's main cemetery on the side of a hill. A simple stone marker with his name and dates. No epitaph. Peter is buried on the opposite hill, same headstone etched with the exact same calligraphy. They may not be buried side by side, but as Viktor said, Isaac and Peter are positioned so that they face one another. Draw your own conclusions.

❖

The grand opening proved not to be that grand. Only Ben, Nina, Olga and Ralf, and, direct from his exclusive engagement at the Turkish baths, "Steam Room Walter." Otherwise, not a single cash-paying customer, a shame given all the trouble Nina had gone to—a large buffet that included several varieties of smoked fish, the obligatory meat pies, and plenty of ice-chilled premium Polish vodka, since they now shunned anything even vaguely Russian.

Several toasts were made to Uncle Leonard and Peter, and one to herald the imminent arrival of Nina and Ralf's child (Sonia was already a week overdue). Then Ben raised his glass high and proclaimed, "to my thick-headed, thin-skinned brother for braving jail and physical violence to realize his cockeyed dream."

I tell you, the guy has a heart as big as Rhode Island.

After a few drinks, Nina, Olga and Ralf treated us to a cappella versions of some traditional songs, plaintive ballads of love, loss, and desolation. You didn't need to know the language to get a lump in your throat. The drunker they got, the louder and more morose the singing became, until one of the neighbors shouted for us to pipe down. Instead, we invited him down to the party along with anyone else hanging by their window. Soon, half the neighborhood was in the café, eating, drinking and straining their vocal cords. One of them even showed up with a little squeeze box.

The evening hadn't turned out like I imagined, but all in all, I considered it a success nonetheless.

As we were closing up, I noticed that Ben had a faraway look in his eyes, probably thinking about his little gamine-for-hire. He'd asked to bring her as his date, and I told him she was welcome any other time, but her presence on opening night might give the wrong impression about our establishment. I hoped he wasn't developing an unhealthy fixation on Tina, not that he'd be the first man to mistake paid passionate sighs for the real thing. Anyway, who was I to dole out sex advice when one of my guests was a man I consorted with in a steam room?

I'd never seen Walter in clothes before and almost didn't recognize him. He wore a stylish gray summer-weight wool suit, and his mustache was neatly trimmed. I told him he could pass for a foreign ambassador or at the very least a distinguished professor, and he giggled self-consciously like a nervous schoolboy instead of the bricklayer he really is. He barely uttered a word all evening, odd for someone who can be quite gregarious when draped only in a towel.

If only Janusz had been there. Since getting out of jail, I had taken several detours past his house hoping to run into him accidentally, praying that he had a convincing alibi so I could forgive him and we could go at each other like wolves. But his house was completely dark. He'd once mentioned that his family took its annual vacation in August. Maybe they'd gone away early this year.

Why couldn't I stop thinking about him? From the start we had an agreement. I had a life to get back to, and he was about to start his, hardly the best ingredients for romance. Still, I wanted to hold him one more time, which I guess is exactly what the alcoholic says about booze, and the junkie about heroin.

During its first full week of operation, the café had only three paying customers, two of them grannies who'd wandered in by mistake and stayed on to play cards. They thanked us and promised to come again. I was grateful, even if they weren't the target audience. The important thing was that we were open.

Ben asked Olga to help him find a travel agent. It was time to return to civilization, though he was planning a pit stop in Paris "because who knows if I'll ever get off my fat ass to cross the Atlantic again."

I assured him his ass wasn't all that fat, and if he kept jogging, it might someday be presentable.

"I'll have you know many of my girlfriends think I have cute *tuchus*."

"For a gorilla, maybe," I conceded.

Though he never introduced me to Tina, when Ben and I said good-bye at the boarding gate, I noticed a young woman in a trench coat with an Audrey Hepburn bob standing over to the side. Don't ask me why Ben would take a prostitute to Paris. Coals to Newcastle. Bagels to Zabar's.

We kept our good-byes formal, as if we'd clicked a switch and returned to our former indifferent selves. Or maybe it was because we wanted to preserve our memory of the past couple of weeks, the one time in our lives that we actually got along, more or less.

By the middle of its third week of operation, the café began to show signs of life. Olga, in the spirit of genuine atonement, redoubled her efforts to draw in the gay crowd. University students were trickling back to town for the fall semester, and she managed to lure a few fey boys and a handful of decidedly un-fey females with the promise of free drinks.

Then, for a few days, business at the café had to take a backseat. After a protracted labor at home, with a midwife and no drugs, Sonia delivered a seven-pound baby girl. Nina and Ralf immediately spirited the child away and christened her Mata. Nina said the baby was named after me, not the

World War I Dutch exotic dancer and spy. Though Olga was chosen to be the godmother, Nina apologized that she couldn't ask me to be an official godparent. Ralf's uncle, the bishop, had put his foot down, something about needing to raise Mata "in the faith." One of Ralf's brothers functioned as my stand-in. I didn't care. At the very least, Nina won half the battle by convincing Ralf to let her "closest friend" serve as godmother. By now, I figured, he was either hip to their relationship or just plain dumb.

In consideration of the fact that Nina had never requested or received a salary—the tips, as you can imagine, were meager—I offered her and Ralf the empty downstairs apartment rent free. This way she could pop across the hall and check up on Mata whenever she wanted. Ralf, as usual, was not consulted in this decision, though after she manipulated him into agreeing, Nina graciously gave him credit for the final decision. Just like any other marriage.

Mata's arrival was a delightful distraction. We each took turns caring for her, though I could sense Olga was leery at first. "You can't stand not being the center of attention, can you?" I chided her.

Again it was Nina to the rescue. She pretended to be all thumbs around the baby so Olga could step in and save the day. The normally taciturn Ralf was a regular magpie around his infant daughter, carrying on lengthy one-way conversations about his plans for her future and how she would never want for love and attention. I understood very little of what he actually said, but the gist was unmistakable. I will admit to shedding a tear, wondering if there would ever come a day when the likes of me or Olga would be able to legitimize our affections and, if we chose, to raise children with our respective spouses. I quickly snapped out of my pipe dream. *Seriously, Matt. Let's lower those expectations, shall we? Being gay became legal here like two minutes ago, and even back home we're regarded as little better than pedophiles and promiscuous plague carriers.*

By mutual agreement, Sonia did not visit the newborn for the first few weeks, giving Mata a chance to bond with her parents. Nina graciously kept her up to date on the baby's sleep patterns, eating habits, and the minutiae of her bowel functions. Why this was a subject of fascination eluded me.

Apart from defraying all the daily expenses for running the café, my responsibilities included closing up shop shortly before midnight. One evening, as I was hauling trash bags to the curb, I heard footsteps behind me.

My stomach started doing backflips as I tried to steel myself for the confrontation I'd been craving and dreading. When I turned, there he was, standing under the portico, a cigarette flickering blue-red. He acknowledged me with a nod, and instead of lashing out, all I managed was a deflated sigh.

"I hope you are well," he said. "Congratulations on the café. You were expecting more people, I know, but you are not always a realist."

Perhaps not the best opening line, I thought, but held my tongue. I could almost see the beads of sweat pop out across his forehead as he tentatively continued. "I am embarrassed for my behavior, but I do not apologize. It would be foolish and not sincere. You knew the chance you were taking."

"So you came by to gloat?"

"No. Just to explain I did what was necessary to protect myself."

"Which included letting me rot in a jail cell?"

"This is not true. Why would I break the door to your home to find the telephone number of your friend?"

"You're the one who called Caroline?" I had always assumed it was Olga or Nina, though neither had taken credit for it.

"Yes. After I call her, I tell my parents we take vacation early because I am in some danger."

"*You* were in danger?"

"I know they will free you because your government would make complaint."

"I guess that lets you totally off the hook."

"I do not know what this 'hook' means, but please try to understand. My future could be ruined even if they think we are only friends. Not just the career. I cannot be certain, even with new government, that they do not arrest me and even Olga and Nina and Ralf. We would be disgraced. Our life would be finished."

"You're the one who assured me that the secret police are gone."

"I believe this to be true. But the memory is still there. You cannot understand such things. But I at least expect sympathy from you. Maybe I make mistake."

This was where I should have extended the olive branch. But I didn't. "Yeah well, we all make mistakes," I said and turned on my heel.

"If I come to café, will you not allow me to enter?"

"It's a free country now, even if you haven't quite gotten the message. Besides, I probably won't be here. I'm leaving in the next few days."

It was a lie. I hadn't booked my flight yet.

But at that moment I knew I was finally ready to go home.

Chapter Twelve
Long(ing) Island

Two years later, I returned to Eastern Europe and sold the café and the apartment building.

But first, home sweet home.

There's nothing like a few months in tumultuous exile in a former Soviet satellite to make northern Long Island seem like a tropical oasis. After going through customs at JFK, my first stop was a newsstand where I stocked up on Tic Tacs, Hershey's chocolate, and the six-pound Sunday *New York Times*.

Home at last.

Caroline was waiting at the curb and immediately climbed all over me. After I finally disentangled myself, she regained her composure enough to observe, "You've lost weight and your complexion is pasty. Next time you have a need to skip town, consider Aruba. That's where I would have gone if I'd been widowed."

"I can just see you in a big floppy straw hat, dyed Indian muslin, and huaraches."

"It's the only proper way to grieve," she said flippantly as she dumped my bag in the trunk.

"Thanks, but I wouldn't have traded in my adventure for a luxury spa in Tahiti."

"Get in. I want to hear everything, especially about your time in the clink. Was it totally gruesome? What kind of prison outfit did they make you wear? Orange? Black and white horizontal stripes? Did you have to bust rocks on a chain gang with swarthy, sweaty men?"

"Yes, but only in the porn version." I sneered.

❖

After so many months gestating in the womb of a tiny one-room apartment, I'd forgotten how intimidating a large, empty house can feel. Within minutes, I started to panic. So I made a quick call to AAA to jump-start the Volvo and drove to the overlit diner where Nathaniel and I connected on that first night almost nine years earlier. The place had changed names several times over the years, usually to reflect the ethnic background of the new owner: Brantley's, Miklos', Rodrigo's. The food, however, was the same scrumptious, all-American, artery-clogging roadside fare. As an appetizer, I ordered blueberry pancakes, then moved on to eggs over medium, with a double rasher of extra crispy bacon, home fries drenched in ketchup, and whole wheat toasted buttered and jammed. And for dessert, two helpings of rice pudding. Throughout the meal I engaged in a long-overdue conversation with Nathaniel, who was sitting right across from me in the red vinyl booth in absentia. This being New York, no one batted an eyelash.

When I returned home, sated and exhausted, I luxuriated in the folds of Egyptian cotton sheets and a down quilt in a bed that was much too wide for one person. Next morning, on my way out the front door, a shingle conked me on the noggin, a clear signal that my neglected home was pleading for attention. Upon closer inspection, I could see why. The summer sun had peeled away patches of paint here and there.

Several wasp colonies had taken up residence under the eaves. Swollen windows refused to budge, and as for the front lawn, if they handed out prizes for mousy taupe strands scattered with dandelions, I would be knee-deep in gardening awards. But after refurbishing a café in a remote pocket of Eastern Europe, this would be child's play. The difference between getting repairs done over there and stateside was that no bribes were required. Our workmen overcharge up front and only show up if the mood strikes them.

For most of the following week, even with both feet firmly planted on American soil, psychically I was still in an intermediate state floating somewhere over the Atlantic. After a few days behind a teacher's desk, though, I finally came back home. The energy I needed to cope with two dozen seven-year-olds five days a week, as well as their sometimes clueless parents and frustratingly small-minded school administrators, roused me from my stupor. How comforting it was to be surrounded by all that raw, spirited young life. And while each day was a series of small disasters and fleeting victories, I had little downtime for morose self-reflection.

On weekends, Caroline dragged me to Manhattan or the local multiplex to catch me up on theater, movies, museum exhibits. Bless you, Caroline. I don't think I would have survived the first anniversary of Nathaniel's death without you.

Next time I looked up, it was summer, and I had two too many months of freedom. I started to miss my little atelier with the big bathroom and the constant aching pain on the bottoms of my feet from walking on cobblestones and even the greasy, tasteless meat pies and stews. I started saving my pennies for a return visit.

I arrived the following summer during the first week of July in the midst of an unprecedented heat wave. A great deal—and nothing—had changed in the interim. My original conception for the café had consisted of Olga handling the finances with Nina assuming the duties of hostess/waitress. Turns out, I'd cast the right actors in the wrong roles. Nina displayed the perfect temperament for running a business. She was tough-minded with a mile-wide streak of pragmatism, the ideal person to drive a hard bargain with suppliers and manage the stress of day-to-day operations. Olga is more like me, impetuous and easily gulled—a fatal combination in commerce. But she is a natural born kibitzer and cajoler. The qualities I had originally found so endearing also beguiled the customers, who were now plentiful. Her bulldog physique also came in handy on the rare occasion the services of a bouncer were required.

By the end of its first full year in operation, Café Eisenhower was a local sensation, though not exactly as the gay meeting place Olga and I had envisioned. I'm not doling out faint praise here, nor am I taking undue credit for its success, except maybe for the café's retro look, which was favorably commented on as far away as the capital.

The nature and appeal of the café had evolved in unpredictable ways. Shortly after my departure, two young musicians stopped by and asked to audition. While Olga and Nina found their sound quite pleasing, they informed the young men that they were wasting their time. The café was barely meeting operating expenses and there was simply no budget for entertainment. No matter, they said. All they wanted was a venue and were quite content to pass the hat. Nina tactfully inquired whether they objected to playing for "artistic" types (and you thought we invented that little euphemism). We accept applause and tips from anyone, they assured her.

One of young men played jazz guitar, and though he was a little raw at first, by the time I saw him perform, he'd worked up some smooth licks and was well on his way toward a pseudo-Django fluidity. The other guy was your standard scruffy, bearded folk singer, who also fancied himself a bit of a poet. Despite his gaunt pallor, he was rather soulful in that long-suffering way that women and even a few men find irresistible. His repertoire featured traditional folk songs that had been discouraged and sometimes banned by the Soviets and were currently undergoing a renaissance as part of an overall explosion of nationalism. Audiences were encouraged to join in, their voices swelling with pride and trembling with emotion. On warm nights, when the doors were open, some of the neighbors sang along from their upstairs windows, a touching celebration of unity and rediscovery.

The performers drew a decidedly mixed crowd that eventually included even some more conservative types. The eclectic makeup of the clientele enabled the queers to hide in plain sight. Among the regulars was Walter, who slowly let down his guard, though he usually spirited his conquests back to the steam room at the Turkish baths. Old habits.

The musicians' popularity had a ripple effect. Revenue more than doubled every three months, and after the first year Nina could finally offer them a stipend in return for exclusivity. In another world, Nina would have made a terrific talent agent. The local newspapers wrote about the café, asserting that its existence presaged the dawn of a new, more cosmopolitan era for the city. Not one of them spelled Eisenhower correctly. They alluded to the "mannered" nature of some of the patrons, but not in a disparaging way, almost as if they were bending over backward to renounce the moral strictures of the Soviet years. Given the cyclical nature of ingrained prejudice, I wondered how long before the inevitable backlash. But for now, anyway, the thaw held.

In addition to being the hostess with the mostest, Olga graduated from university with honors and was invited to join the faculty in a junior professorial position. She also became a celebrated local author—well, not an author so much as an editor. While juggling classes, with her duties at the café and helping care for Mata, Olga still managed to carve out time to finish translating Uncle Leonard's notebooks, which contained at least one major revelation that gave us all a jolt.

When she discussed her work with both gay and straight patrons, they encouraged her to edit the original notebooks into a book-length narrative. One of the regulars ran a local imprint and, after reading a couple of chapters, agreed to publish it. Fittingly, the book was offered for sale at the very café in which some of the events took place. Olga conducted several readings, which were very well received, and the book flew off the counter. By its third printing, it had received praise from several local critics and as with the café, the book's publication was offered as proof that democracy had successfully taken root. There was also the titillation factor. The depiction of forbidden love, while modest by Western standards, was considered quite provocative. The book's title roughly translated as *A Bittersweet Romance of Two Very Different Men* by Anonymous, didn't exactly trip off the tongue, but it certainly piqued interest.

A publishing house in the capital approached Olga about acquiring the rights to distribute the book nationwide, where it fared decently and was similarly well received. As expected, the church and the right wing raised a stink, which always has the unforeseen effect of stimulating sales.

Somehow, no one ever made the connection between the book and the café's clientele, which might have brought out the skinheads, whose numbers had multiplied in my absence, to the point that the local government was finally forced to push back. The police were under considerable pressure to keep extremist groups in check since the city was trying to revitalize its tourist trade, which included massive infrastructure repair and a small building boom. The Belle Epoque train station was in the process of a meticulous restoration, as were a couple of my favorite river bridges, several town squares, and the three major parks, including the misbegotten Luna Park where the freshly painted horses were placed back on their perches and merrily went round and round. I'm told that the cruising crowd returned as well, a little younger and a little less desperate.

I let Olga and Nina keep all profits from the book, which they poured back into the café, though I retained all rights outside Eastern Europe. I hope to someday find an interested buyer, and I must come up with a less cumbersome title.

Nina finally 'fessed up to Ralf about her feelings for Olga. He didn't blink. Fine, he scoffed, you can have your little schoolgirl crush, but I'm in love with Sonia and I can't live without her. The man to whom Sonia had been promised was, by now, out of the picture. I'm not sure whether she flat-out turned him down or just happened to mention she'd recently given birth to another man's child. Hey, the heart wants what it wants.

Neither Ralf's uncle the bishop nor his parents would agree to let him divorce Nina. They preferred a Noel Coward–like agreement that seemed to please everyone except Sonia's parents, who disinherited her and moved to the mountains to escape their shame. Ralf and Sonia moved up to my old apartment while Nina and Olga set up house in the downstairs flat with Mata. But if anyone asked, Ralf and Nina still lived together and Sonia and Olga were spinster roommates.

Once he got his jaw working again, Olga's brother Alexei departed for the former East Germany to live with his estranged dad. He was missed by no one. Then Nina told Ralf she wanted to conceive and hit him up for a donation. Sonia, who was not interested in being pregnant again, gave Ralf her blessing. It took several tries but they toughed it out. I guess no one's ever heard of turkey basters in Eastern Europe.

A boy, Leonard, was born shortly before I arrived.

With the rapidly expanding nuclear family, they had little room for me, so I had to make do on a trundle bed in the café after it closed, though I didn't always sleep alone. I met several university-age young men who saw me as—gulp—a daddy figure. I half expected them to ask for my AARP card. I became quite taken with a Polish-born German student named Ludovic, who had a brilliant mind. He was actually studying to be a rocket scientist or something of the sort. Ludovic was tall and ruddy and cosmopolitan, achingly gentle and devoid of any noticeable neuroses. His English was flawless, and he could devolve into complete silliness at a moment's notice.

"You should remain here and live with Ludovic," Olga said one night as we left the town's new first-run theater, where we'd sat through Scorsese's *The Age of Innocence*. "He is a kind man, not arrogant like Janusz."

"You just don't want me to go back home," I answered.

"Is true. But Ludovic will make you happy, like me and Nina."

"Ludovic will also probably move back to Frankfurt, and where would that leave us? I might be willing to share my life with someone of Slavic origin, but I would never consider living in Germany. Ludovic says I need to work on that. Maybe I will. Maybe I won't."

In mid-August, after tearful good-byes to my adopted niece and nephew and a promise to visit Ludovic the following summer in someplace neutral like Switzerland, I stopped in Amsterdam on my way home. Janusz and I had begun a correspondence soon after I returned to the States. He eventually apologized for having dissed the café. "No one of us would have had the courage to make this leap of faith," he wrote. "It might have taken another twenty years. Your uncle and Peter are looking down upon you with favor."

After graduation, Janusz had been hired as a clerk in his country's embassy in The Hague but left after only a few months to join a forward-thinking trade organization that was developing international business opportunities in Eastern Europe.

With greater exposure to the outside world, Janusz no longer found my opinions outré and came to regard his own as decidedly provincial. In turn, I tried to make amends for my intransigency, admitting that I sometimes behaved like the prototypical American bully. I refused to take credit for Café Eisenhower since its route to success was circuitous. And whereas I might have at one time been skeptical of Nina and Olga's have-your-cake-and-eat-it-too arrangement with Ralf and Sonia, just as with the café, I now viewed it as a small step toward greater liberation. Maybe Mata and Leonard's generation will be able to live openly. I have my doubts. Like anti-Semitism and racism, homophobia is a fairly intractable prejudice, a convenient and reliable go-to distraction in times of political uncertainty.

During my very stoned week in the Netherlands, I told Janusz I still had feelings for him. And it wasn't just the awesome weed talking. He had made great strides. His fear and self-righteousness had abated somewhat, and he was freer and more willing to test his limits now that he lived in a more broad-minded corner of the world. In the two years since I'd seen him, he'd gone through the obligatory sexual kid-in-the-candy-store phase and recently had his heart broken by a West Indian man who proved to be faithless. "It was terrible, it was wonderful," he said of his ill-fated affair.

A few months later he visited me in New York. I gave him the cook's tour of Manhattan, then we embarked on a long weekend trip to New England. When I was with him, I didn't know how I'd be able to stand not having him around. Inexplicably, now that we're apart, I don't think about him that much.

Ludovic writes me every week, the kind of love letters everyone should get at least once in their lives, serious and dripping with youthful ardor. There's nothing lewd about them, but they still make my pulse race. Janusz would never allow himself to be that emotionally naked, and I doubt that even Nathaniel would have been able to compose this kind of mash note, at least not with a straight face. For Nathaniel, the friendship was as important as the romance. With a little more life under his belt, I suspect Ludovic will come to a similar pragmatic conclusion and transfer his affections to someone who doesn't live on another continent. I hope it's not before next summer, when we've decided on Venice, where I'm determined to overpay for a romantic gondola ride.

My brother Ben and I may never be close, but our little sojourn in the old sod was a breakthrough. We have dinner together whenever I'm in the city, and I invited him to a Fourth of July picnic at my house. Though it was a mixed crowd and no one lisped or pranced, Ben said it was still a little too gay for him. When I asked him to categorize "a little too gay," he simply said, "You know what I mean." Since the conversation would likely go around in circles and I'd wind up hitting him with a frying pan, I decided to let it drop. The real reason I asked him to come was to introduce him to Caroline. They seemed to hit it off and went on several dates. Then she stopped returning his calls. "The only kind of prince I'm interested in," she explained, "is one with a real title and a castle."

Ben is now seeing someone and says they may get engaged. She's very much a carbon copy of all the other girls he's dated. While he would never cop to it, I think he fell in love with Tina. I was right, by the way. They did spend a week together in Paris. He said it was one of the most memorable weeks of his life even if she did insist on being paid for her time.

❖

A new teacher named Simon took over fourth grade this fall, substituting for the regular teacher, who's on maternity leave. He's odd and kind of gawky in an appealing way, and very funny. He has a crush on me, and I think I may have one on him too. We haven't dated yet, however. Too awkward given the work situation, we've agreed. Still, I fantasize about doing the nasty with him. He says that next September he'll be taking a full-time position at a school two towns away and, if we're still interested, we'll give it a go. Hopefully by then, I will have finished unpacking all my emotional baggage and placed it in storage, and will be ready to consider sharing my life with someone who lives in the same time zone.

I still eat at the diner at least once a week where Nathaniel and I play catch-up. He is of the opinion that my experience in Eastern Europe was beneficial because it exposed me to several different tiers of love. There was the heightened level I shared with him, bounteous and fulfilling though unfortunately attenuated; then there was the indissoluble commitment between Uncle Leonard and Peter (see Notebook Six below), which survived oppression and long separations. He went on to discuss my deep affection for Olga and Nina, and even Caroline, each of them more than friendship, almost kinship.

The relationship between Olga and Nina (and Ralf and Sonia) was intense and all-consuming, he said, yet required subterfuge, accommodation, and understanding. The emotional ties I had to Janusz were secure when we were together but curiously fragile when we separated. I felt protective toward Ludovic, whose regard for me was near devotional, and that, too, would likely evolve into something different, though as with Janusz it seemed restricted by geography. Closer to home, Simon was a definite possibility. Our attraction percolated under the surface and could come to a boil should we decide to act on it.

"See how lucky you are, Matt? Who knows how many other gradations and varieties of love you will be exposed to over your lifetime," Nathaniel says, leaning over the table.

In my sense memory, I can almost feel the warm kiss he plants on my forehead.

NOTEBOOK SIX (1960)

The rewards of being in each other's company after such a long separation are enough to sustain Isaac and Tonio for a time. They content themselves with all-too-brief daily visits. Drinking greedily from each other's cups, they nonetheless maintain a respectful distance and are careful to avoid any discussion of feelings deeper than friendship. Both are mindful of Tonio's responsibilities as a husband and father, and the fact that they are living under the thumb of a stringent and unpredictable regime in which the slightest deviation from acceptable behavior could be denounced. Since new restrictions and prohibitions are introduced on a monthly basis, they are loath to do anything that might jeopardize their renewed acquaintance.

The long-term effect of Tonio's war injuries leads to a slow but progressive decline in his general health. He is no longer able to sustain the ten- and twelve-hour work days at the haberdashery, and with scores of healthy young men eager for his position, he is mindful that Pyotr, his employer, will not abide such limitations indefinitely. Pyotr has put off dismissing him because Tonio is otherwise a first-rate salesman, cordial, inviting, and effective. The ladies who frequent the shop are devoted to him. He flatters them and caters to their every whim, even on the days when he is crushed by exhaustion and plagued by debilitating headaches.

True to his promise, Tonio carves time of out of each day to see Isaac, even if it is just for a brief cup of tea or a glass of beer at a local tavern. Isaac is concerned about Tonio's steady downward spiral but takes great pains to mask it. To do otherwise would be a blow to his friend's pride. Tonio puts up a brave front, making light of his afflictions and pretending he doesn't see the flashes of panic in Isaac's eyes whenever his wounded leg cramps and he is unable to completely stifle his cries of pain. Despite his alarm, Isaac continues speaking as if nothing out of the ordinary had occurred. Tonio appreciates the gesture. He would do the same if the situation was reversed.

Finally, after one too many missed workdays, Pyotr begrudgingly relieves Tonio of his position. In a way, he is grateful to be dismissed. Now he will be spared the indignity of his employer and customers watching him deteriorate in public. As he gathers his belongings and bids farewell to Pyotr, thanking him for the opportunity, he tells himself that he and Isaac will come up with a solution. He is sure of it.

Isaac has been quietly preparing for such an inevitability, lying in wait for an opportune moment to announce his rescue plan. He has rehearsed his speech thoroughly in the hopes that when the time arrives, it will come out without effort, as if the idea had just entered his mind. The difficulty in achieving this kind of calculated spontaneity gives him a newfound respect for the acting profession.

That evening, Tonio pulls himself up the two flights of stairs, arriving at Isaac's door in a more winded condition than usual. A look of defeat is so solidly etched on his face that he despairs of concealing it from the one person who can read his soul. He needn't have bothered to pretend, because the moment Isaac opens the door, he surmises the truth. As he sits Tonio down in an armchair and serves him a cup of tea and a piece of buttered bread, Isaac feigns distraction. What is the matter? Tonio asks. Forgive me, Isaac says, but before you tell me about your day, I was wondering if I might discuss with you a matter of great urgency.

On any other occasion, Tonio would have easily seen through Isaac's ruse. But he is so addled by his own troubles that he is only too happy to delay discussing them. I can see that something is bothering you, he tells Isaac. Please, you know you can speak freely with me.

Isaac clasps his hands together as if in thanks for an answered prayer. He confesses to Tonio that he has committed a foolish blunder. Without telling anyone, he has purchased a property—two apartments and an adjacent carpentry shop. The selling agent assured him that the rent from the apartments and the shop would be more than sufficient to cover his monthly expenses, even if he chooses to live in one of the flats himself. Only after signing the papers does he learn that he has been deceived. The current tenants are paying a ridiculously low rent as mandated by the government. Further, the carpenter recently died and his son has no intention of carrying on the business. Isaac fears he may be facing financial ruin.

Why have you not spoken of this to me before? Tonio asks, though he is already suspicious as to the timing of Isaac's announcement. Moreover, he has never known his friend to be so rash or impetuous. Isaac says he has delayed any mention because their time together is always so fleeting. He had been meaning to bring it up but was too ashamed to admit how easily he'd been outwitted. A childish reaction to be sure, he tells Tonio, but there it is. He was also hoping that in the interim, he might come up with a practical solution. Then he could entertain Tonio with the story of his near catastrophe, and they could both enjoy a good laugh at his expense.

Then, Isaac continues, as if by divine intervention, he has had an inspired idea, though it is risky to be sure. Before I outline it for you, he says, I must preface it by saying that my plan has no chance of succeeding without your cooperation. I realize that this is a great deal to ask of anyone and be assured in advance that I will not be offended if you refuse. But first hear me out, dear friend, and promise you will give it serious consideration.

Isaac launches into his rehearsed speech, trying his best to make the words seem effortless. A possible way out of his dilemma, he says, is to repurpose the carpentry shop as a men's club, a haven for the locals, a cross between a beer hall and a gaming establishment—chess and cards. It would open in the late afternoon to attract men on their way home from work; a place to stop for a drink and socialize. He has already petitioned the local authorities for the proper permits, to which they have consented provided that he employ government-approved tradesmen and agrees to include at least one war veteran among his employees.

Though he has already tipped his hand, Tonio plays along. It is not a bad idea, he tells him. But what does this have to do with me?

Well, you see, if I was to open such an establishment, I would need a host, someone with an easy nature whom I could trust, and you are the ideal candidate in every respect. Moreover, you are a veteran, which would satisfy the authorities. I would also like to assure you that the job would not be strenuous. I would only need you in the afternoon and evening. I plan to bring on a server for the drinks and the prepared food, sandwiches mostly, and to bus the tables. But anyone can be a waiter. It takes a particular kind of person to be a host.

Tonio is touched by the lengths to which Isaac has gone to take his feelings into account so that the offer doesn't sound like charity.

I see that you hesitate, Isaac says, when Tonio doesn't immediately respond. You can be sure I will pay you well. I would never take advantage of our friendship. No, indeed, your salary will be at least equivalent to what you currently earn, and for fewer hours. Eventually, if the venture prospers, and with your participation I have every confidence it will, I will increase your salary accordingly. Otherwise, I would never ask you to consider leaving a secure position for such an uncertain one.

Again, Tonio is amused, but also relieved. Now he can return home to his wife with some good news to temper the bad. Alla will undoubtedly complain that he's placing his future in the hands of someone she barely knows, but when confronted with the alternative, she will surely capitulate.

Tonio asks if he might take a day to discuss the proposition with his family. Since this is a matter of some import, he says, I don't want to give a hasty answer. The truth is that if he were to accept on the spot, given the stress of the day, he might embarrass himself and break down in front of Isaac.

Of course, take your time, Isaac says. Although I must confess that my motives are not entirely pure, given that if you take the position, I will be assured of your company for several hours every day, and nothing in this world would give me greater pleasure.

What an odd dance we are engaged in, Tonio thinks. Isaac must be aware that, in the deepest recesses of his being, he would realign the planets for the chance to be with him on a regular basis. In the most aloof voice he can command, Tonio thanks Isaac, adding that the opportunity for closer contact would certainly be a consideration in his decision.

Before you leave, Isaac asks, aren't you going to tell me what happened today? Oh, Tonio replies, as he pulls himself up, the usual nonsense. Not even worth mentioning.

❖

Working alongside Isaac in the café has a salutary effect on Tonio's health since he is able to rest in the mornings and spend most of the evening seated on a high stool behind the counter, rising only to greet the patrons and perhaps join a party at one of the tables, to chat, tell jokes, and sometimes even play a hand of cards. The blinding headaches from the shrapnel embedded near his brain are also less pronounced. Though Tonio does not believe in psychology, he is forced to concede that this sudden turn for the better cannot be due merely to an unanticipated physical reversal. The joy of being in daily contact with the only person he has ever loved must account for some of the change. It most certainly has had a beneficial effect on his demeanor.

As Isaac suspected, Tonio is an ideal host, attracting a steady and loyal clientele. The evenings are always busy, particularly in summer. In addition to the regular waiter, during school holidays Tonio's son Dag is brought on for a few hours. Isaac pays the boy a generous stipend and sometimes sneaks him a few extra coins. He takes a genuine liking to Dag, who gradually breaks through his initial wariness, undoubtedly fostered by his mother. As time passes, Isaac develops a rapport with the boy and is confident that he has earned his respect at the very least.

There is no such hope with Alla, though he holds no rancor toward her. Since Isaac first appeared in their lives, she has sought to undercut the friendship. Predictably, she opposed her husband taking the new position even after Tonio informed her that he had been dismissed from the haberdashery. After she spoke her piece, he informed her that the decision was not hers to make and regardless of her feelings, he planned to accept Isaac's generous offer.

Tonio does not mean to be dismissive of his wife. He keeps in mind that life has not been kind to her either, and that the future she was promised has been dashed. Their union was supposed to enhance the standing of both their families. She was not at all displeased with Tonio, finding him handsome, intelligent, and good-natured. Her father reassured her, and she saw no reason to doubt him, that once the war was over, a suitable position in the government would be secured for Tonio, one offering the potential for significant advancement. With his winning personality and keen mind, there was no limit to how far Tonio might rise, perhaps even on a national level.

The false sense of security into which she had been lulled proved to be short-lived. Calamity followed upon calamity, starting with Alla's difficult pregnancy. Her son Dag was born prematurely. Just a month later, before Tonio had even seen the sickly newborn, he was seriously wounded. In addition, what little help her and Tonio's families had provided came to an abrupt halt when the Russian army occupied the town. Soon after, Tonio's father took his life and her own beloved papa was summarily executed without trial, shot in the back of the head as he sat at his desk. Both families fell into disgrace. Had the war lasted another year, she and Dag would likely have starved to death.

While many others had suffered similar or worse fates and survived to stoically face the future, Alla was not a resilient woman. She regarded every misfortune as a personal affront.

Her undisguised disdain only compounded her husband's woes.

Though he would never admit it to Isaac, Tonio was secretly grateful that his friend had not contacted him when he first returned. If he had, Tonio would have immediately abandoned his wife and son and gone off with him. But in the interim he had grown attached to Dag and now felt responsible for him—and, by extension, the boy's mother, a woman he did not love and who offered no kindness or affection.

❖

At the café, Tonio and Isaac now spend half the day in each other's company. Yet the more time they are together, the more painful their separation each evening. After the café closes, Tonio usually loiters, finding any excuse to remain. It is only at Isaac's insistence that he finally boards the last bus home shortly after midnight. Even if he is not finished cleaning up, Isaac locks the doors and accompanies Tonio to the bus stop and, if necessary, helps him up the steps. Tonio wishes, just once, that Isaac would forget to look at his watch and let the bus go past. But Isaac knows that if that happens, it wouldn't be for just one night. If Tonio shared his bed even once, Isaac would never let him leave.

Tonio's health problems aside, he and Isaac are still in the prime of life, vital and spirited. They share the same appetites and find satisfaction only in each other. Not acting on their desires inevitably leads to tension. At times it is as difficult for them to be together as to be apart. Petty quarrels arise and are left to linger unresolved. Neither is willing to confront their steadfast, unyielding need for one other, which only exacerbates the problem.

On a particularly warm summer night, as Tonio is closing the shutters and extinguishing the lights, Isaac removes his shirt, rolls up the cuffs of his pants, and starts to mop the floor. Tonio has been especially distant all day, even in his interaction with the patrons. Isaac attributes it to the heat or perhaps a lingering migraine. When he expresses his concern, Tonio curtly rebuffs him. Isaac shrugs it off, but at the same time finds himself losing patience with his friend's erratic behavior. Earlier in the day he suggested Tonio take a few days off to rest up, to refresh himself. Tonio looked right through him as if he had spoken but no sound emerged. If you like, I'll be more than willing to compensate you for your time off, Isaac informs him. Please do not make me insist. I am in no mood to argue.

As Isaac is attempting to remove a frustratingly stubborn patch of grease from the tile floor in the kitchen, he senses Tonio behind him. Before he can turn around, Tonio pushes him up against the wall and presses against him with the strength and determination of someone trying to subdue a dangerous intruder. The wind knocked out of him, Isaac struggles to wriggle free of Tonio's grasp. Let me go, Isaac screams. Have you lost your mind? But Tonio holds fast, and Isaac is forced to jab an elbow into his stomach. Tonio doubles over, but quickly recovers and comes at him again, slamming Isaac to the floor.

A temporary insanity comes over Tonio, and it soon infects Isaac as well. As their bodies commingle, they tear at each other like wild animals, without the slightest tenderness or affection. When it is over, they seem to fall into a restless sleep, from which they revive some time later only to go at each other again, this time with even more ferocity. At the end, covered in blood and sweat, they fall asleep on the kitchen floor.

When Isaac awakens the next morning, Tonio is gone. He rouses himself and, still naked, walks through the café, locks the door behind him, and never sets foot inside again.

SOME YEARS LATER circa 1976

Dag is a grown man the next time Isaac sees him. He is on his bicycle, stopped at a corner where he is speaking to another young man, most likely a friend, Isaac surmises as he monitors the conversation from across the road. As they chat, Dag surreptitiously reaches under the tarp draped over the basket of his bike, and there is a quick exchange.

When the man walks off, Isaac calls out to Dag, who turns with a start. Then, recognizing him, Dag breaks into a smile. It is so good to see you, uncle, he says, and they shake hands. Isaac is struck by how closely Dag resembles Tonio at the same age, just around the time of their separation. He is unsettled by how vivid that distant memory still seems. He is also saddened by the thought that if faced with the same decision today, he would have chosen to remain and enjoy whatever time was left to him. Death would have been preferable to his current non-existence.

Dag, what a wonderful surprise, Isaac says. You've grown into quite a handsome young man. Tell me news of you. Are you at university? What are you studying? Is there a girl?

Head bowed, Dag replies that he has not been able to continue his schooling. Father is no longer able to work, he tells Isaac, and his veteran's pension is barely enough to put food on the table. Isaac is at a loss for words and, just as he regains his voice and is about to ask his address so he might pay a visit, Dag glances over his shoulder and speeds off without saying good-bye. Isaac turns and notices a policeman rounding the corner.

It is Alla who answers the door. When she sees Isaac, she tries to close it again, but he stubbornly barges into the tiny, unheated basement flat. Tonio is napping in a jerry-rigged wheelchair, which is merely an armchair attached to two bicycle tires. Propped up against it are two sturdy wooden canes. Alla clicks her tongue at him disparagingly and Isaac turns on her sharply. I have come to tell you to pack your things. A van will be here in the morning. You and Tonio and the boy are moving into my home.

With you? Alla scoffs. No. That will never happen.

Listen, woman, Isaac continues, undaunted. I am the head of this family now, and you will do as I say. We are going to live under the same roof, and I want no argument. When we are settled, the boy will return to finish his studies. I am determined that he not end up in prison. And don't pretend you don't know what I'm talking about.

Isaac takes out his wallet and holds out several bills to Alla. Now go and get us some decent food and come back and make dinner. Alla doesn't budge. Isaac reaches for her coat, which is hanging on a peg, and forces her into it. He jams the money into her hand and pushes her out the door.

When he turns around, Tonio is gaping at him. He is frail and appears perhaps ten years older than his actual age. There is no particular look of surprise on his face, almost as if he'd been counting the days.

Hesitantly, and in a reedy voice, Tonio begins. Friend, there is a question I have been meaning to ask you for the longest time. What is this need we have to punish each other for the very feelings that have always sustained us?

Isaac crouches down on his haunches, steadying himself on the armrests of the makeshift wheelchair. That is all in the past, he says. I promise you, and you must believe me, that until we are in our graves, we will never be apart again, not for a day, not for an hour.

Alla proves to be a terrible cook, so Isaac assumes those duties. Except for the occasional misunderstanding, Alla, Isaac, and Tonio co-habit in relative harmony. Her resentment, while palpable, remains in check. While Isaac is at work, she cleans the house and shops for groceries. In the evening, after dinner, Alla washes the dishes while Isaac bathes Tonio and dresses him for bed. Depending on how tired they are, the two men read to each other for an hour or two, usually adventure stories—Dumas, Kipling, Alger, Patrick O'Brian—many of which they know almost by heart. Occasionally, they listen to music, mostly opera or American jazz. Afterward, Isaac carries Tonio to bed and then retreats to his room to grade papers, though in later years, when his health is also on the wane, he almost immediately falls asleep.

Dag completes his studies, meets a young woman, and starts a family. Though he is still loyal to his mother and sympathetic to her discontent, he is nonetheless respectful of Isaac and grateful to him.

Despite the constant headaches, Tonio's mental faculties remain intact. To keep himself occupied while Isaac is at work, he begins writing journals, recollections, stories, observations. Whenever he finishes a volume, he shows it to Isaac. They never discuss the contents. It is like a private correspondence, words with special meaning only for the two of them. Only years later does Isaac break this silence, reciting a particular passage that caught his eye and that he has since committed to memory. He repeats it frequently, particularly on the evenings when the headaches or the pain in Tonio's legs is almost unbearable.

"If there had been no war, I fancy we would have run off together, become merchant seamen and seen all the places we had promised ourselves we would visit back when we were boys—Istanbul, Rio de Janeiro, Shanghai, New York. Seeing them through each other's eyes would have enhanced the experience, doubled our delight. Most of our lives, though, would be spent on the open sea. And that is where we would find our true rhythm. At night, after completing our duties, we'd stand against the deck railing and converse, reliving the exotic sights and odd customs we had witnessed, always discovering a new insight or observation. Then, when words were no longer required, we would fall into a mutual silence and gaze out at the sea which, for us, would be forever calm. We would stand there shoulder against shoulder and contemplate the ever-elusive horizon."

Now, Isaac says softly as Tonio drifts off, imagine we actually lived that life and that at this very moment, we are standing on that deck together—today, tomorrow, always.

About the Author

Richard Natale is a writer and editor whose work has appeared in such publications as the *New York Times*, the *Washington Post*, the *Los Angeles Times*, the *Village Voice*, and *Variety*. He has published two prior novels, *Junior Willis* and *The Golden City of Doubloon*, and a short story collection *Island Fever*. Additionally, he wrote and directed the feature film drama *Green Plaid Shirt*, which played at more than 20 festivals around the world. He won the National Playwright's Competition for the comedy *Shuffle off This Mortal Buffalo*, which was produced in Los Angeles and Kansas City. His short stories have appeared in such publications as *Wilde Oats* and *Chelsea Station*. Natale may be contacted on Facebook at Richard Natale Author Page.

Books Available From Bold Strokes Books

Café Eisenhower by Richard Natale. A grieving young man who travels to Eastern Europe to claim an inheritance finds friendship, romance, and betrayal, as well as a moving document relating a secret lifelong love affair. (978-1-62639-217-5)

Balls & Chain by Eric Andrews-Katz. In protest of the marriage equality bill, the son of Florida's governor has been kidnapped. Agent Buck 98 is back, and the alligators aren't the only things biting. (978-1-62639-218-2)

Murder in the Arts District by Greg Herren. An investigation into a new and possibly shady art gallery in New Orleans' fabled Arts District soon leads Chanse into a dangerous world of forgery, theft...and murder. A Chanse MacLeod mystery. (978-1-62639-206-9)

Rise of the Thing Down Below by Daniel W. Kelly. Nothing kills sex on the beach like a fishman out of water...Third in the Comfort Cove Series. (978-1-62639-207-6)

Calvin's Head by David Swatling. Jason Dekker and his dog, Calvin, are homeless in Amsterdam when they stumble on the victim of a grisly murder—and become targets for the calculating killer, Gadget. (978-1-62639-193-2)

The Return of Jake Slater by Zavo. Jake Slater mistakenly believes his lover, Ben Masters, is dead. Now a wanted man in Abilene, Jake rides to Mexico to begin a new life and heal his broken heart. (978-1-62639-194-9)

Backstrokes by Dylan Madrid. When pianist Crawford Paul meets lifeguard Armando Leon, he accepts Armando's offer to help him overcome his fear of water by way of private lessons. As friendship turns into a summer affair, their lust for one another turns to love. (978-1-62639-069-0)

The Raptures of Time by David Holly. Mack Frost and his friends journey across an alien realm, through homoerotic adventures, suffering humiliation and rapture, making friends and enemies, always seeking a gateway back home to Oregon. (978-1-62639-068-3)

The Thief Taker by William Holden. Unreliable lovers, twisted family secrets, and too many dead bodies wait for Thomas Newton in London—where he soon enough discovers that all the plotting is aimed directly at him. (978-1-62639-054-6)

Waiting for the Violins by Justine Saracen. After surviving Dunkirk, a scarred and embittered British nurse returns to Nazi-occupied Brussels to join the Resistance, and finds that nothing is fair in love and war. (978-1-62639-046-1)

Turnbull House by Jess Faraday. London 1891: Reformed criminal Ira Adler has a new, respectable life—but will an old flame and the promise of riches tempt him back to London's dark side…and his own? (978-1-60282-987-9)

Stronger Than This by David-Matthew Barnes. A gay man and a lesbian form a beautiful friendship out of grief when their soul mates are tragically killed. (978-1-60282-988-6)

Death Came Calling by Donald Webb. When private investigator Katsuro Tanaka is hired to look into the death of a high profile lawyer, he becomes embroiled in a case of murder and mayhem. (978-1-60282-979-4)

Love in the Shadows by Dylan Madrid. While teaming up to bring a killer to justice, a lustful spark is ignited between an American man living in London and an Italian spy named Luca. (978-1-60282-981-7)

In Between by Jane Hoppen. At the age of fourteen, Sophie Schmidt discovers that she was born an intersexual baby and sets off on a journey to find her place in a world that denies her true existence. (978-1-60282-968-8)

The Odd Fellows by Guillermo Luna. Joaquin Moreno and Mark Crowden open a bed-and-breakfast in Mexico but soon must confront an evil force with only friendship, love, and truth as their weapons. (978-1-60282-969-5)

Cutie Pie Must Die by R.W. Clinger. Sexy detectives, a muscled quarterback, and the queerest murders…when murder is most cute. (978-1-60282-961-9)

Going Down for the Count by Cage Thunder. Desperately needing money, Gary Harper answers an ad that leads him into the underground world of gay professional wrestling—which leads him on a journey of self-discovery and romance. (978-1-60282-962-6)

Light by 'Nathan Burgoine. Openly gay (and secretly psychokinetic) Kieran Quinn is forced into action when self-styled prophet Wyatt Jackson arrives during Pride Week and things take a violent turn. (978-1-60282-953-4)

Baton Rouge Bingo by Greg Herren. The murder of an animal rights activist involves Scotty and the boys in a decades-old mystery revolving around Huey Long's murder and a missing fortune. (978-1-60282-954-1)

Anything for a Dollar, edited by Todd Gregory. Bodies for hire, bodies for sale—enter the steaming hot world of men who make a living from their bodies—whether they star in porn, model, strip, or hustle—or all of the above. (978-1-60282-955-8)

Mind Fields by Dylan Madrid. When college student Adam Parsh accepts a tutoring position, he finds himself the object of the dangerous desires of one of the most powerful men in the world—his married employer. (978-1-60282-945-9)

Greg Honey by Russ Gregory. Detective Greg Honey is steering his way through new love, business failure, and bruises when all his cases indicate trouble brewing for his wealthy family. (978-1-60282-946-6)

Lake Thirteen by Greg Herren. A visit to an old cemetery seems like fun to a group of five teenagers, who soon learn that sometimes it's best to leave old ghosts alone. (978-1-60282-894-0)

Deadly Cult by Joel Gomez-Dossi. One nation under MY God, or you die. (978-1-60282-895-7)

The Case of the Rising Star: A Derrick Steele Mystery by Zavo. Derrick Steele's next case involves blackmail, revenge, and a new romance as Derrick races to save a young movie star from a dangerous killer. Meanwhile, will a new threat from within destroy him, along with the entire Steele family? (978-1-60282-888-9)

Big Bad Wolf by Logan Zachary. After a wolf attack, Paavo Wolfe begins to suspect one of the victims is turning into a werewolf. Things become hairy as his ex-partner helps him find the killer. Can Paavo solve the mystery before he runs into the Big Bad Wolf? (978-1-60282-890-2)